Save
The
Gator
Queen

To Rachael, + Kiersten Happy Reading! Jeffery Lamb

Jeffery Lamb

ISBN: 0-9760453-1-1

For questions or comments about this book, or to order
more copies. E-mail the author at:
savethegatorqueen@yahoo.com

A special thanks to:

Vickie Hall for her editing help

And

Art Roscoe and Brian Riolo for
their illustration on the cover

Dedication

To my mother, the only proof I have that angels walk this earth.

CHAPTER 1

"Kylee, wake up. Kylee! Wake up!" her mother said, pulling the covers off of her.

"What time is it?" the fourteen year old girl said as she raised her head, her long blonde hair covering most of her face.

"It's almost four o'clock. Your dad is waiting down stairs. C'mon get up."

"Four o'clock?"

"Yes."

"In the morning?"

"Yes."

"Mom." Kylee fell back over in bed.

Kylee was not looking forward to this summer. Sure it was better then being in school but she was not excited about spending it at her grandmother's in Central Florida. She loved her grandparents but didn't want to leave her friends, or her dog behind. Also, there was the five or six

1

hour ride from Pensacola to Ocala that was not on her list of favorite things to do.

Kylee drug herself out of bed and got dressed. She threw a couple more pairs of shorts into her open suitcase and another pair of socks before heading down stairs.

"Hey mom, what if I promise to call Grandma Sheila every day, then could I stay here for the summer? Please." She said entering the kitchen.

"Listen Kylee, I've told you a hundred times now that you have to spend the summer with my parents because your uncle Ray has lost almost everything in the last hurricane. We have to do all we can to help him. You are too young to stay here by yourself for the whole summer."

"Aunt June only lives two blocks from here; I could stay with her." Kylee pleaded.

"You know your Aunt June works nights and I don't want you left alone after dark. She has agreed to take care of Skip while were gone, and we should be thankful for that. Now finish getting packed. Your father wants to be on the road as soon as you're ready so get a move on." Her mother smiled at her as Kylee hung her head and mumbled something.

"Ok mom, but I wish I were a dog so I could stay with Aunt June." Kylee slumped her shoulders forward and headed back to her bedroom. Her father came in from outside.

"Alright I think we have just about everything loaded in the car," Larry Bowman said.

"Everything except for your daughter, she's not happy about leaving her friends behind for the summer," Sandy Bowman said as she put her arms around her husband's neck.

"How come when there is a problem with Kylee she is my kid, but when everything is going fine she's our kid?" Larry started to laugh; his lovely wife did not see the humor in his comment. "Ok, ok I'll go talk to my daughter." He pulled away from Sandy's embrace and headed up the stairs.

After having a short talk with her father and putting a few more things into her suitcase, Kylee gave Skip a hug goodbye and they were on their way to the Ocala National Forest.

"I've got to go to the bathroom." Kylee said from the back seat of the Bowman's two door car at it traveled east on interstate 10.

"You got to be kidding me," her father said from behind the wheel. "We just left the house forty-five minutes ago."

"I'm just saying I have to go," Kylee answered.

"Didn't you go before we left home?" Larry asked.

"Yep."

"And you have to go again already?"

"Yep."

"Just take the next exit Larry, and we'll be back on the road in no time." Sandy said calmly.

"This is going to be the longest trip ever." Larry said looking at his wife.

"Well, we don't have a plane to catch; we're in no hurry." Sandy reached over and touched Larry's arm.

"This is going to be the longest trip ever." He looked in the rear view mirror at Kylee as he said it this time.

"Yep," Kylee said with a smile. Her father turned on his blinker and got off at the next exit.

Seven hours later the Bowman's car was turning into the Shady Oaks Mobile Home Park along the edge of the Ocala National Forest, "*Where you really start to live.*" At least that's what it said on a sign next to the road, but Kylee didn't see it as they pulled in. She was sound asleep in the back seat.

"Kylee we're here!" Her mom reached between the seats and gave Kylee's leg a good shaking. She opened her eyes just in time to see six or seven mobile homes that all looked exactly the same as they slowly passed by her window.

"Thanks for waking me mom; I wouldn't want to miss a minute of this." Kylee sat up rubbing her eyes; her mother was too busy looking for Seagull Lane to respond.

"Turn left right here, Larry. This is it!" Sandy said with excitement in her voice. She had not seen her mother in over two years. Larry turned left and ran over the fifth speed bump since they had entered the small park.

"There it is, right there, the white one with the porch swing in the yard." Sandy was pointing up ahead to the right.

"That could be any of them; they are all white with a swing in the yard." Kylee said staring at little white mobile home after little white mobile home.

"Alright now Kylee, that is about enough out of you young lady, you be good this summer and don't upset your grandparents." Sandy's voice lost its cheerfulness.

"If you're going to get mad at me, what did you wake me up for?" Kylee kept her voice low enough not to be heard.

"Sandy, she has a point. Every house I've seen

has been white." Larry said pulling into the driveway. Sandy looked around, they did all look alike.

"Just be on your best behavior this summer, alright." Sandy saw her mother coming down the steps of her home. "There she is, there she is!"

Kylee was happy to see her grandmother too, just not for the whole summer.

"Oh my, I can't believe they're here! Jack, hurry up, they're here!" Grandma Sheila was running as fast as a sixty eight year old woman could run.

"Mom!" Sandy was out of the car as soon as it came to a complete stop. The two women were hugging in front of the porch swing before Kylee even had the car door opened.

After some iced tea and a short visit, Kylee and her grandmother were waving good-bye to her parents from the porch swing.

"Well, it looks like it's you, me and grandpa for the rest of the summer honey. We are going to have so much fun." Sheila said as she put her arm around Kylee's small shoulders and squeezed harder than was necessary.

"Yeah fun, I can hardly wait for all the fun to begin." Kylee watched her parents' car disappear down the lane. Just as it did, a green pickup came

6

toward them and stopped in front of the mobile home across the street. A small jolly looking woman came quickly out of the screen door wiping her hands on the apron she was wearing.

"Justin's here! Oh Justin you're here, I can't believe it!" She shouted.

A tall thin boy got out of the truck; he looked to be a couple of years older than Kylee.
He had short spiked hair and was wearing blue jean shorts and a Tampa Bay Buccaneers t-shirt.

"Hi grandmother, I'm so glad to be here!" He said grabbing a backpack and a skate board out of the back of the truck.
"Oh brother, what a liar this kid is." Kylee thought to herself. She watched as they went inside the house.

"Why don't you and I go and bake some cookies?" Sheila said as she got up off the swing. Kylee hung her head.

"Ok grandma." She said as she thought about all the fun her friends must be having together back home.

CHAPTER 2

The sun was shining brightly the next morning as Kylee rolled out of the small bed tucked away in her grandparents' spare bedroom.

"Morning." She mumbled as she slowly ambled into the kitchen.

"Hey sleepy head, it's about time you get up." Her Grandfather Jack said. He seemed much happier than a person his age should be, she thought. "I've been waiting for you to wake up all morning to see if you want to walk down to the lake with me and see if we can catch something for lunch." Jack put his hand on top of her head and shook it gently.

"I don't think so grandpa, I'm no good until I get a couple of hours of cartoons in me." Kylee sat the pitcher of orange juice back in the refrigerator and shuffled toward the table. Sheila gave her a sharp look and nodded toward Jack. Kylee rolled her eyes.

"I mean, sure grandpa just let me eat and get dressed." For some unknown reason grandma could get anyone to do whatever she wanted them to do and no one seemed to know how she did it.

"Good, good. I'll go get an extra fishing pole rigged up for you." Jack said and headed out the back door to the shed.

"That'll make your grandfather so happy; he's always wanted someone to go fishing with." Her grandmother smiled at her.

"How come you don't go with him?" Kylee said under her breath.

"What dear?" Sheila slid a scoop of scrambled eggs onto Kylee's plate.

"I said, how could I resist fishing? Yeaaa!" Kylee put some ketchup on her eggs, and then stabbed them with a fork.

She ate quickly and changed out of her pajamas and was soon sitting on a dock watching a small red and white bobber floating on the surface of Clear Lake next to her grandfather. If she was home, she could think of a hundred things she could be doing with her friends right now, and none of them had anything to do with fishing.

Two hours later, with only one bite that got

away an Kylee was about to scream from boredom. Grandpa Jack had been asleep now for the last half hour when the boy from across the street came walking down the path. He sat down on the other side of the dock and started baiting his hook with a freshly dug worm.

"Catch anything?" He asked her over his shoulder.

"Yea, I caught a headache from staring at the sun glaring off the lake." Kylee answered in a low tone, not to wake up grandpa. Justin jerked hard on his pole and began to quickly reel in his line. An eight inch fish was dangling from the hook.

"Hey, how did you do that?" Kylee said looking at the fish flopping around on the dock. If she had to sit there all day, she might at well try to catch something. "We've been down here all morning and haven't caught a fish yet." She stood up and walked over to where he was sitting.

"What are you using for bait?" Justin asked.

"I don't know, grandpa put it on for me." She swung the small minnow on the end of her line within inches of his face. He glanced up at it and continued putting the fish he had caught on a stringer, then tied it off to the dock.

"He must have got them at the bait house up the road. They're usually half dead when you buy them. You need something with some wiggle in it." Justin grabbed the line as it swung by his head again and took the barely breathing minnow off and threw it into the lake. He shoved his hand down into a coffee can sitting beside him and came out with a big fat worm and quickly threaded it onto her hook. "There try that." He said, letting go of her line.

Kylee gave the pole a half-hearted cast out about ten feet away from the dock. She stood quietly for just over a minute before her pole took a dip toward the water. She pulled back hard.

"I got one! I got one!" She took off running up the dock dragging her pole behind her.

"Stop! Stop running!" Justin scrambled to his feet just as a small fish fighting for its life flew past him. Kylee stopped and turned toward him as he caught up with the fish and picked it up off the dock. "All you have to do is reel it in, not take off running." Justin wiped the poor little fish off on his shorts and then handed it to one of the strangest kids he had ever met.

Kylee took the fish over to where her grandfather, was surprisingly still napping, and put it in the bucket beside him. She walked back over to Justin, who without a word, took hold of her line and put another worm on its hook. She didn't cast

11

it this time. She just looked at him as he stared at his bobber on the shimmering water. What a strange kid, she thought.

"What's your name?" She said, as he sat back down.

"Justin." He answered.

"I'm Kylee, where you from?"

"I live in Orlando but I always spend the summer out here with my grandmother." Kylee's mouth dropped open.

"So you come out here in the middle of nowhere on purpose. Why?" She couldn't believe a kid would be out here because they wanted to be.

"I like it out here, fishing and wandering through the woods. It's so quiet and peaceful." Justin took a pack of cheese crackers out of his tackle box and offered her one. She took one from the pack and popped it into her mouth whole.

"Who wants quiet?" Kylee asked, after a few chews.

"Well, probably anyone who spends much time around you for one." Justin said with a laugh.

"That's not funny." Kylee snapped back. "Although you're not the first person to ever say that to me. Oh well, so you plan on spending the whole summer stumbling through the forest and sitting here on this dock fishing, huh?"

"No, that's not all. My grandmother has a friend that has a boat and he's going to let me use it, so I won't be sitting on the dock all summer but I will be fishing."

Justin just wanted to be left alone all summer, he was happy to be away from all the kids at school. He liked being by himself, unlike Kylee who couldn't be the center of the attention if no one was around to pay attention to her.

"Well, that's about the dumbest plan I've ever heard. You're lucky I'm here this year. I'll find some fun stuff for us to do." She sat down on the dock next to him. He stared at the water.

"Kylee! Kylee, where are you?" Jack said, waking up.

"I'm over here grandpa," Kylee fiddled with her fishing reel. "This is my new friend Justin." Justin shook his head; he didn't want to be friends. He wanted to be left alone and not have to talk and answer questions all the time.

"Hello there Justin," Jack said standing up. "You're Lucille's grandson that lives across the street from us aren't you?" He gathered up his fishing equipment and came over to where the kids where sitting.

"Yes sir, I think we met last year." Justin said shaking Jack's hand.

13

"Oh yeah, that's right I remember now. Well Kylee I think we better get going."

"You go on grandpa; I'll be up in a little while." Kylee said turning her attention back to the lake.

"We'd better go home together or I'll be in trouble with your grandmother. I think she wanted you to help her bake some pies for the Gator Festival this weekend. You don't want me in trouble with grandma, do you?" Justin was glad to hear that.

"No, I wouldn't want that." She stood up and reeled in her line. "Do you want your worm back?" She dangled it in front of Justin's face again.

"Yeah, thanks." He took it off the hook and threw the mangled worm into the water, thankful that she was leaving and he could get some serious fishing done.

"I'll see you soon," she said.

"Oh good, I can't wait," Justin said. This is going to be a long summer he thought.

CHAPTER 3

Kylee helped her grandmother in the kitchen the rest of the afternoon making homemade pies for a bake sale.

"Why is the whole trailer park having a bake sale? I thought you only did that when you were in school." Kylee asked, as she finished sifting some flour.

"It's to raise money for the annual Gator Festival, and it's a mobile home park not a trailer park," Sheila answered.

"What's the difference?" Kylee asked.

"I'm not sure, but I know the people that have lived here a long time don't like it to be called a trailer park." Sheila took another pie out of the oven.

"Oh, ok. What's a Gator Festival?" Kylee responded.

"Almost every town around here has some kind

of festival or parade. Twenty-five years ago Dewey Martin, he was a judge at the time, he's retired now, decided we should have our own festival, even though we're not a real town. He set up his bar-b-que grill down on the beach and told everyone in this part of the woods to come and have some fun. We didn't live here at that time, but I heard that the smell of all that fried chicken caused all the alligators to swim to that area of the lake. That's how it got it's name the Gator Festival. They had to cut the party short because everyone got scared that they would be attacked.

"Were they?" Kylee asked but didn't really care either way.

"No, but from then on, everyone comes together the first weekend in June to celebrate. It's got so big now we even have a parade and everything." Sheila picked up a mixing bowl.

"It's too bad the gators didn't attack." Kylee plopped another spoonful of whipped cream on top of a pie.

"Now why would you say that?" Sheila asked.

"Because if the gators would have attacked, it would have made it a much better story. Don't you think?" She smiled.

"Kylee Bowman, don't you talk like that." Sheila threw a dish rag at her granddaughter.

Save the Gator Queen

"So, where's the parade route? There's not a main street within ten miles of this place.

"We run from the volunteer fire station just north of here down the highway to Deer Creek Road. It runs straight into the forest about three miles then circles back out right across from the park here."

"Grandma, the road across the street is dirt." Kylee said.

"That's right." Sheila pulled another pie from the oven.

"Ya'll have a parade down a dirt road?

"It's not really dirt, its clay. And yes, we do."

"You can't have a parade on a dirt road. No one will come." Kylee couldn't believe what she was hearing. She had heard sometimes older people lose their minds, but she didn't think it could happen in her family.

"We have people come. You would be surprised if you knew how many people lived out here in the middle of no place."

"Really? Well, how many floats did they have in the parade last year, grandma?" Kylee was listening more carefully now. Her line of questioning was designed to see if she needed to call grandpa in from the swing so he could run to the drug store and get some kind of medication for

17

grandma.

"We don't really have floats. We have a fire truck, a hearse, some golf carts, and Dewey usually rides his three-wheeled bicycle. Sometimes we have a Boy Scout troop and stuff too. Oh, I almost forgot the most important part."

"Let me guess the U.F.O from Mars." Kylee said laughing.

"Don't be silly." Sheila said.

"Who me?" Kylee said, pointing to herself. "I'm not the one putting on a parade that no one will see." Her grandmother ignored the smart remark.

"I forgot to tell you about the Gator Queen." Kylee fell off her barstool with laughter.

"Gator Queen? What's a Gator Queen?" She picked herself up off the floor. She wrapped the dish rag around her head and batted her eyes at her grandmother.

"Look at me grandma, I'm the Gator Queen."

"Young lady, now that is about enough out of you." Sheila was trying to keep from laughing herself.

"The Gator Queen is the most important thing that has come out of the Gator Festival. You see each year we elect a Queen to represent the people who live out here in the forest. It started out as a goof."

"You're kidding." Kylee butted in but was ignored.

"That was until two years ago when we elected Grace Stevenson." She stared at Kylee.

"What! I don't know who Grace Stevenson is." This might be a good time to yell for grandpa she thought.

"Grace Stevenson is famous out here in the woods."

Famous in the middle of nowhere. Boy, what an honor! Kylee thought, but was too afraid to say it. This hit Kylee as odd also, because she was never at a loss for words.

"Piney Hillville!" Sheila shouted.

"Grandma, your scaring me." Jack came in the door just in time. "Grandpa help, grandma is losing it."

"What is she screaming about?" he said, concerned.

"Piney Hillville!" Sheila shouted again. Kylee quickly turned to her grandpa.

"Piney Hillville! No to Piney Hillville!" Jack shouted back at his wife.

"Stop it!" Kylee decided it was her turn to scream. "Who is the Tiny Hillbilly?"
This seemed to bring Sheila out of her trance.

19

"Not Tiny Hillbilly." She said calming down. "Piney Hillville." She pulled up another barstool and sat down. "A big development company wants to build an upscale community on all the land around Clear Lake and Crystal Lake. All the plans were in place and construction was going to start in a few months. Everyone around here was going to have to move because they were going to take all of the land for their golf course community they wanted to build. That was until Grace Stevenson was elected as Gator Queen. Kylee have you ever heard of The Church of The Turkey Frog?"

"The church of who?" Kylee was completely lost. None of this made sense to her.

"Well, there is a legend in this area of a frog that has feathers on its back and can fly short distances," Sheila said seriously. "People who believe in the turkey frog, believe it has magical powers. People like Grace Stevenson. There is a small group of these people and they meet out in the forest on the 13th of every month to give thanks to the great turkey frog. They are known as The Church of The Turkey Frog." Sheila looked at her granddaughter, unable to believe she had nothing to say.

"Anyway, Grace went to the county court house and lobbied that the construction had to stop because the endangered turkey frog would be killed off."

"So they stopped a housing development because some crazy woman complained about a flying frog?" Kylee spoke at last.

"Not at first, because the frog was not on the endangered list, so Grace went on a frog hunt for two weeks."

"And what did the wonderful Gator Queen find on her frog hunt?" Kylee was pleased to have the ability to make a snide remark again.

"No one but her knows for sure, but she did produce a video tape." Sheila took two glasses out of a cabinet and filled them with iced tea.

"And what was on the tape?" Kylee took a sip of her tea.

"A frog, a frog with feathers." Sheila smiled.

"So it was a fake?"

"Nobody knows. Nobody knows but Grace, but it was enough to cause an investigation into the turkey frog that is still going on and it's been almost two years now," Sheila smiled.

"So the government has people out in the woods looking for a flying frog?" Kylee asked.

"Yep and they keep finding strange evidence that the frog may exist." Sheila said.

"Grace is planting evidence?" Kylee asked, but

her grandmother just shrugged her shoulders.

"That was two years ago and you'll never guess who the Gator Queen is this year."

"Grace?" Kylee asked again.

"Nope, it's Holly. Grace's younger sister. So you see why the Gator Festival and the Gator Queen is such a big deal, because without it we would have had to move away from this beautiful area." Sheila thought she was going to cry.

"Here's to the new Gator Queen." Kylee said as she raised her glass into the air. Sheila clinked her glass to her granddaughter's.

"Here's to the Queen," she said.

CHAPTER 4

The sun was sinking behind the tall pines as Kylee plopped down in the porch swing. She heard a door slam and quickly turned around to see Justin running down his driveway.

"Where are you going?" She asked as he headed up the street.

"Mr. Preston said I could use his boat all summer, but I have to get it tonight because he is going out of town in the morning." Justin said. He wasn't sure how hard it was going to be to drag a twelve foot aluminum boat to the lake, and a little help might be nice. "You want to come help me?" he asked her.

"Hang on. I'll go see if I can." She ran in the house so fast that she was in the door before she even finished the sentence.

"Grandma! Grandma, can I go with Justin to help him get a boat? It won't take long and I'll be careful, please." Kylee said while running through the small home.

"Slow down dear. What are you talking about?" Sheila put down her crossword puzzle and looked over her reading glasses.

"Justin borrowed a boat from some guy and he needs me to help him get it to the lake."

"Who is Justin and where did he get a boat?" Sheila asked. Grandpa chimed in.

"He's Lucille's grandson across the street. They must be talking about Joe Preston's boat over on Palm Street." Jack said.

"Yea, that's it, Preston's boat. Can I please?"

"Oh I don't know Kylee, it's going to be getting dark soon and I…"

" Sheila, she'll be fine." Jack said.

"Oh all right, go ahead." Sheila looked at her husband but he just kept his eyes on the television.

"Thanks grandma," Kylee said.

'Don't thank me, thank your grandfather." Sheila answered.

"Thank you grandpa!" she shouted as she ran out the door. Justin rolled his eyes when he saw her jump off the porch at full speed. What have I gotten myself into, he thought?

"Ok, I'm ready to go." she said when she met up with him in the street.

"Great." He started up the street.

"So what kind of a boat is it?" she asked, and then continued before he could answer.

"How big is it?"

"Does it have a motor?" Kylee bombarded Justin with questions.

"How far away does this guy live?"

"Do you know how to drive a boat?"

"We need to turn here," was the only thing Justin said the whole trip, thinking maybe he should have come alone.

"Are you going to go out on the lake tomorrow?" Kylee waited this time for an answer. Justin waited for more questions. It was the first three seconds of silence since they had left her house.

"Well, are you?" she asked again.

"Yea, I'll probably take it out tomorrow sometime." he answered.

"All right! Do you think we can go all the way across the lake with it?" Kylee said. Justin didn't answer.

"Well do you?" Where did she get we from, he thought? I never said anything about us going fishing.

"You don't talk much, do you?" Kylee ran ahead of him and was now walking backwards in front of Justin.

"No, not compared to you, I guess I don't." She made a goofy face at him. He started to laugh.

"Yeah we could probably make it across the lake if we wanted to." he said.

When they reached the right address, Justin went up and knocked on the door. Mr. Preston walked around to the back of the house with the two teens. He was a very tall man and was very friendly to them.

"There it is." he said pointing to a small green boat pulled up on the shore. Mr. Preston's house backed right up to Clear Lake. To Justin's surprise a tiny old outboard motor was mounted on the back of the boat.

"Wow! I didn't know it had a motor on it." Justin said.

"I just bought that at a yard sale a couple of weeks ago. Do you know how to operate an outboard?" Mr. Preston asked.

"I have run them before but not very often." Justin said, not believing his luck.

"You're not going to get us killed with this thing are you?" Kylee said, putting her hands on her hips. Mr. Preston laughed.

"Is this your little sister?" He asked.

"No, thank God. No relation." Justin answered

quickly.

"We're just best friends for the summer." She put her arm around him because she knew it would embarrass him.

"Well, you don't have to worry about this little motor," Mr. Preston said putting his hand on it.

"It will get you around the lake but you won't be breaking any speed records with it."
He showed Justin where the gas shut off valve was and how to choke the carburetor. Justin paid close attention while Kylee kept slapping at mosquitoes.

"Also, take this pad lock and chain and you can lock it to the dock over near your grandparents' place. Just steer around the lake this way and it's the first dock you come to." Mr. Preston pointed and then helped Justin move the boat into the water.

"I thought we were going to drag it home." Kylee said hopping into the front of the boat before it was floating.

"We didn't know you lived right on the lake." Justin said to Mr. Preston. "If I'd have known this, I would have come alone." The two of them pushed the boat and its passenger deeper into the lake.

"What is this for?" Kylee said, lifting a small anchor. "Hey, how do you steer this thing? "Do I have to wear this?" she picked up a life jacket.

"She was like that all the way over here," Justin said. Mr. Preston laughed. Justin looked at Kylee; she had found a bag of rubber worms in the bottom of the vessel and was holding them up like she was afraid of them.

"Kylee I'll explain everything to you later. Right now just sit still." The boat began to float as he climbed past her to get to the motor. If Mr. Preston thought they didn't know what they were doing, he might change his mind about them taking it.

"Thank you Mr. Presley." Kylee waved as Justin started the motor and turned the boat in the right direction.

"It's Preston, You goofball! His name is Mr. Preston." He asked her to come so he would have some help and now he might not get the boat at all because of her, he thought.

"Oh ok, sorry Mr. Preston." She hollered then turned to Justin. "Then who is Mr. Presley? I know I've heard that name before."

"You're thinking of Elvis Presley," Justin said. Kylee turned to look at him.

"Who?"

"Elvis Presley. The singer, you know," Justin sang part of '*I'm all shook up*'. "You know."

Justin said wiggling his shoulders and trying to crinkle his lip.

"You're weird." Kylee said, and then faced the front of the boat.

Justin steered the boat with little difficulty around to the dock where he had first met his 'best friend for the summer' and padlocked the small boat to a post then climbed up on the dock where Kylee was already waiting.

"Good job Captain. You got me here safe and sound." She said, giving him a salute then put her hand on his shoulder.

"You're lucky we didn't see any alligators or I would have pushed you in." Justin said shoving her hand away.

"We probably didn't see one because your singing must have scared them all away, Elvin."

"It's Elvis, Elvis Presley! Everyone knows who Elvis Presley is." Justin said gesturing with his arms.

"Oh yea, right, whatever." She said.

Kylee, get up here right now. You had me worried to death!" Sheila was walking down the path toward them as fast as she could. Kylee turned to see her.

"What, you said I could go." She said, thinking her grandmother had forgotten and she was in trouble for no reason.

"I know I did, but we just got some news and I think you need to come inside for the night. Justin you should probably get home too." Sheila stopped at the edge of the lake and waited for the kids to come toward her.

"Why, what's going on." Kylee asked.

"Carol, a friend of mine just called. Her husband is a deputy sheriff and he told her that Holly Stevenson is missing and they think that she may have been kidnapped." She took Kylee by the hand.

"Who is Holly Stevenson and why would anyone kidnap her." Justin asked.

"Because she is Grace Stevenson's little sister and she is also the new Gator Queen." Sheila said, her eyes darted about as she spoke like she was telling them a secret and didn't want any one else to hear.

"Oh brother, here we go with the Gator Queen talk again," Kylee said walking next to her grandmother towards home.

CHAPTER 5

Justin woke up late the next morning. It was almost eleven o'clock before he was out the door and headed to the lake.

"Justin, before you go fishing would you bring in the newspaper at the end of the drive way please?" his grandmother asked.

"Sure grandma, I'll go get it," he said through the screen door. Justin picked up the paper and saw a picture of the most beautiful girl he had ever seen on the front page. He read the caption under the picture wrapped in a clear plastic bag. **Local Beauty Queen Missing.**

"About time you get out of bed. I've been waiting for you on the swing for almost an hour," Kylee said walking up to him.

"What made you so sure that I hadn't already gone fishing before you came out?" he said.

"Because I went down to the dock and saw the

Titanic was still sitting there. That's how." Kylee twirled one of her long blonde pig tails.

"What, are you stalking me or something?" Justin asked.

"I just thought it would be best if we look out for each other since we're the only two kids around and there's some crazy kidnapper on the loose."

"What are you talking about?" Justin said.

"It's right there on the front page silly. Someone has kidnapped a seventeen year old girl and she only lives about three miles from here." Kylee put her hand on the paper in Justin's hand.

"How do you know where she lives?' Justin asked, looking at the picture again.

"Because my grandmother told me all about her last night and that I should be careful so that it doesn't happen to me."

"I wouldn't worry about it if I were you. After an hour or so they would bring you back." Justin said, laughing at his own joke.

"Ha ha, you're so funny." Kylee pushed the newspaper up toward his face but he was able to stop it before it hit him.

"Hang on a minute, let me take this in to my grandmother and then we'll go fishing," he said and ran up the driveway. Kylee entertained herself by watching a line of ants making it's way in a northern direction as she waited. Justin came back carrying a couple of fishing poles and a tackle box.

"Ready?" he asked.

"Yep, I want to try to catch a swordfish so I can hang it on my wall back home." Kylee said taking one of the poles.

"You're not going to catch a swordfish in a lake, you can only catch them in the ocean." Justin said shaking his head.

"But what if I'm a really good fisher...um...person, then I could catch one." Kylee tried to give the rod a quick snap like she had seen on TV but the rod slipped out of her hands and sailed fifteen feet down the street in front of them.

"Oh yeah I see what you mean now. You might catch a swordfish, maybe even a whale." Justin said, starting to worry a little about being in a small boat with her all day.

"A whale, don't be ridiculous." She said and ran to pick up the fishing pole. "The wall in my room is not big enough to hold up a whale." she laughed.

Sheila and Jack were sitting on their porch drinking coffee when the two teens met up with each other outside.

"It's nice that Kylee has someone close to her age to spend time with this summer." Sheila said before returning to her crossword puzzle. Jack looked up just as the expensive fishing rod went flying through the air.

"Yeah that's good I guess. I just hope she doesn't cause too much damage, we're on a fixed income you know." he said.

"Jack! How could you say that about your own granddaughter?" Sheila scolded him.
He nodded toward the street just as Kylee bent over and picked up the fishing rod.

"We'll you could always get a part-time job if you need to. I know the hardware store in Weirsdale is always looking for help." She looked at her husband and smiled.

The two teens trolled around to several different spots on the lake but were not having any luck at catching fish.

"This stinks." Kylee said sitting her rod down. "I give up. How come you were catching fish last night and we can't even get a bite today?"

"That's just how fishing is," Justin said. 'Sometimes you have a good day and sometimes you don't." Kylee slipped off her shoes and hung her feet over the edge of the boat.

"Don't do that you'll scare them away," Justin said even though he was about to give up on fishing too.

"Scare what away? I think they are all asleep. Let me see if I can wake up a few for you." She kicked her legs hard and fast.

"I don't think fishing is your thing. I should probably leave you behind next time." He reeled in his line and laid the rod in the bottom of the boat. "Are you ready to go home?"

"Nope, I just don't want to fish anymore." She kicked her feet again.

"Ok, let's cruise around a little." Justin pulled the rope on the little outboard and headed the boat in the opposite direction of home. Kylee lifted her feet and centered herself on the bench seat. Justin steered toward the far shore and down a small canal. He cut the motor and drifted into the sandy shore. Kylee stared up at the slight slope in front of her.

"What is this place?" She said.

"I think it used to be some kind of hunting camp or something. I found it when I was out here last year." Justin said.

"Does anybody live there?" she asked looking at the broken down cabin.

"Nah, I don't think anyone has used it in years.

35

It's just got some old junk furniture in it, that's all. Justin carefully worked his way past her and jumped off the bow of the boat onto the shore.

"I want to see the inside." Kylee stood up on the seat and hurled herself onto the shore.

"Alright let's go." Justin said and pulled the boat up on the beach. Kylee headed for the cabin with Justin right behind her. Tall grass and overgrown bushes surrounded the whole structure making it a little difficult to get to. After pushing their way through some pretty thick foliage, while keeping an eye out for snakes, Kylee slowly opened the door. A three legged table with two chairs, one lying on its side, was sitting just inside the door. A thin layer of dust covered everything.

"This is creepy," Kylee said picking up a glass jar then setting it back down.

"What's creepy about it? It's just an old empty cabin." Justin sat the knocked over chair upright.

"I don't know, it just seems kind of spooky." She opened a door that lead into a bedroom.

"It looks about the same as it did last year." Justin kicked a pillow across the floor stirring up a cloud of dust.

"What are you doing? Trying to kill us?" Kylee pretended to wave dust away from her face and coughed. A loud noise came from outside causing

them both to run for the door. Out on the porch
they could see where a giant limb from a nearby
pine tree had broken off and made it even more
difficult to get back to their boat.

"Boy, I'm glad to see that!" Justin said. "I
thought someone was shooting at us."

"Hey, look at this!" Kylee said, picking up a
long thin piece of bright pink satin.

"That's new, wonder where that came from?"
Justin watched her as she wrapped it around her
head and tied it in a knot in the back. She looked at
the limb between them and their boat.

"I'll karate chop us out of here," she said
striking a kung fu pose.

"Oh yeah, ok now I feel better." Justin stepped
off the porch and pushed past the fallen limb.

"Hi yat! Woop woop woop!"The loud sound
came from behind him as Kylee chopped her way
through.

"Back on the boat they cruised out of the canal
and back across the lake.

"Are you going fishing tomorrow?" Kylee
asked as Justin wrapped the chain around the dock
and locked the boat in place.

"I'm not sure. I think I have to help my
grandmother decorate a hearse." Justin answered.

"You got to help do what?" Kylee tilted her

head like a dog that heard a whistle.

"Some guy she knows owns an antique hearse and they decorate it up for the Gator Parade. I guess it's the Shady Oaks float."

"Yeah, I had to help bake pies yesterday for a Gator Festival sale. I wonder what they're going to do about the Gator Queen? I hear she's a pretty important part." Kylee said climbing up on the dock and picking up her fishing rod. Justin shrugged his shoulders. They walked up the path together and down the street.

"Well, I guess I'll see you later." Justin said as Kylee handed him the fishing pole.

"Ok, I'll see you later." Kylee left Justin in the street.

"Hey grandma, I'm hungry. What have you got to eat?" She said and turned on the kitchen sink to wash her hands.

"It's about time you get home. Do you realize how long you've been gone?" Sheila asked while taking a pot of stew out of the refrigerator.

"I told you we were going fishing." Kylee sat down at the table.

"Well it just worries me with everything going on." Sheila put some stew in a bowl and stuck it into the microwave.

38

Save the Gator Queen

"Have you heard anything new about the Gator Queen?" Kylee asked.

"Just that the Volunteer fire department is organizing a search party tomorrow and your grandfather and I have volunteered to help. I think it might be a good idea for you to go with us.

"Sure, I'll help look for the queen." Kylee picked up a spoonful of stew and blew on it.

"After you eat, you better get to bed. We have to meet everyone at six o'clock in the morning," Sheila said pouring Kylee a glass of milk.

"Six o'clock in the morning, on my vacation?" She dropped the spoon back into the bowl.

"It's not going to hurt you to learn how to help other people," Sheila said.

"I don't have anything against helping other people grandma. I just prefer to do it in the afternoon, that's all," Kylee said, then ate her dinner and went to bed.

CHAPTER 6

Jack pulled his car into the fire station at ten minutes till six. Sheila and Kylee climbed out of the car together and made their way across the crowded parking lot. A long table was set up in front of an open garage door of the brick building.

"Hello Jim; This is our granddaughter Kylee. She's going to help out with the search today." Sheila said to a man with a white beard, wearing an Orlando Magic cap sitting behind the table.

"Good! We can use all the help we can get. We have organized three groups that are heading out in different directions." He tore three pieces of yellow plastic off of a roll on the table. "Tie these around your arms; I'm going to send you guys with the yellow group. They are going up near Moss Bluff and then heading back this way." He handed Sheila the strips of plastic.

"Ok Jim, thanks." Sheila said.

"Each group has a group leader and they can radio back to the station here if ya'll come across anything," Jim said. Sheila and Kylee disappeared into the group to find Jack.

"It looks like we are teamed up with The Church of The Turkey Frog." Sheila said as they passed a bunch of people all dressed in black with dark make-up around their eyes and all of them with a piece of yellow plastic tied around their arms.

"I'm sure glad the sun is coming up, wouldn't want to be out in the woods in the dark with them," Kylee said looking back at the people in black.

"Just because someone is a little different from you, does not make them a bad person," Sheila said still trying to find Jack.

"Yeah, I know that; if they are a little different, but would you look at those outfits? All black in the middle of summer, that's weird!" Then from the crowd of people in black she heard her name being called.

"Grandma, they're trying to pull me into their web of darkness! Grandma help!" Kylee screamed. Justin pushed his way through the sea of long black dresses and men wearing trench coats wondering why Kylee was running from him.

"Kylee, hey wait up!" He called out again.

41

"Justin, what are you doing here?" she said and punched him in the arm when he got close enough. "You scared me half to death."

"When I got home last night, my grandmother told me that the hearse project had been called off so everyone could help look for Holly the Gator Queen, so here I am." Kylee saw a blue plastic ribbon around his left arm.

"It looks like we'll be going in different directions," Kylee said holding up her strip of yellow. Justin took it out of her hand.

"Here let me tie it on your arm before you put it around your head and try to karate chop someone. It's bad enough you got teamed up with the weirdoes, you don't want them to think you're one of them, do you?" Justin put her armband in place.

"I'm kind of glad I'm with them. This way, I'm not the odd ball for a change," Kylee said with a goofy smile.

"What are they, some kind of cult or something?" Justin said.

"They are The Church of The Turkey Frog." Kylee raised her hands up and wiggled her fingers at Justin and saw the look of confusion in his eyes. "Long story, if I get out of this alive, I'll tell you all about it." She dropped her hands.

"Kylee, you stop talking like that about other

people," Sheila said, walking up behind her with Jack. "They are here to help just like the rest of us, so that makes them good people. I don't want to hear another negative thing out of your mouth about them. Do you understand me?"

"Oh great and precious Turkey Frog, give us the power of Mother Nature to find our lost tadpole!" The loud chant came from the members of The Church of The Turkey Frog, as they held hands and formed a circle. Sheila's mouth dropped open and her yellow plastic ribbon hit the ground.

"You won't hear a word out of me. They are as normal as we are, right grandma?"
Kylee said.

Jack followed four other cars down the two lane highway toward Moss Bluff. The caravan turned onto a dirt road and traveled a short distance farther before pulling over to the side of the road. Everyone got out of the cars and gathered near the edge of the forest.

"That's Grace over there." Sheila pointed to a very tall girl with long black hair.
She was wearing, a black long sleeve shirt and black pants; with a silver metal belt separating the two.

"I'm so glad all of you could be here today,"

she said turning to facing everyone.

"I know my sister is still alive because the glorious turkey frog came to me in a dream last night and told me so. He will guide us through the wonderful forest today without harm, because of the love for your fellow man that lives inside of each of our hearts. Mother Nature will reward you for giving your time to help find Holly on this beautiful day." She closed her eyes and slowly lifted her arms upwards. "Oh great turkey frog, hop from your palace and guide us safely on our journey through your precious forest. We promise no harm to the woodlands and ask nothing in return. Thank you, oh great turkey frog, thank you." She lowered her arms and took a deep breath.

"Thank you great turkey frog, thank you." The people in black chanted. Kylee was unable to take her eyes off of Grace. The passion in her voice and her slow, smooth movements made her seem like someone to be looked up to.

"You know, I bet there really is a turkey frog grandma," she said to Sheila. Sheila was also staring at Grace.

"I wouldn't be surprised dear," she said.

The group lined up down the road about twenty feet apart and then proceeded into the woods.

Save the Gator Queen

Kylee was between her grandparents but kept looking past her grandfather at the beautiful Grace Stevenson. What was it about her that made her so special and demand people's attention the way she did?

After forty five minutes of walking, they came to a large round clearing with six tall crosses made out of pine trees in a circle. Grace called the search party all to the center of the circle. Between each of the crosses were two small logs with one larger one laid across them to form benches.

"For those of you who have never been here before, this is where the members of the Church of The Turkey Frog meet. We'll take a short break before going on."

"Grace! Grace!" A man in his early twenty's dressed in black came running up to the group.

"Come quick, I found something," he said. Grace wasted no time following the man; everyone else fell in behind her. The young man came to a stop in front of the tallest of the crosses. "Look." He faced Grace and pointed at the cross. Grace slowly walked to where a piece of paper was nailed to it. Everyone stood in silence while she read it. Then she tore it from its nail and turned to face everyone. Anger filled her large green eyes as she scanned the crowd. She jerked the paper up to her face and looked at it. Then she read from it.

"This is a warning to the Church of The Turkey Frog. We have something of interest to you. The only way to get her back would be to admit that the turkey frog is a hoax and allow us to gain the permits needed to proceed with our plans for Piney Hillville. If you comply with our request by Saturday at 10:00 am we will release the Gator Queen before the parade begins. If not, she will become gator bait, so do not hesitate."

Grace folded the paper calmly and then radioed into the station the information. Leaders of the other search groups chatted back and forth on their radios for a few minutes before deciding to call off the remainder of the search.

Kylee's group made their way back to their cars in silence. Everyone hung their head except Grace who held her head high as they walked. Jack drove back to Shady Oaks Mobile Home Park.

"Well, it looks like were going to lose our little piece of paradise after all," he said as he parked the car in the driveway.

"It's not over yet Jack," Sheila said, closing her car door.

"Yes, it is Sheila, because now it's life or death of a young girl. We can't fight that, the stakes are too high this time," he said, not wanting to give up but not knowing what else to do. Justin and his grandmother pulled into their driveway as they stood there by their car.

"We heard about the ransom letter." Justin said coming across the street.

"We were there when they found it," Kylee answered. "It was kind of scary; the letter was nailed to a big cross where The Church of The Turkey Frog meets at."

"Yeah, my grandmother told me a little about them. They looked like a bunch of freaks. So I guess you fit in nicely, huh?" Justin gave Kylee a little push. "So you want to go fishing for the rest of the day?"

"They are not freaks, they are really good people and I like them," Kylee said stepping toward Justin. He stepped back.

"Ok ok, I'm sorry." He put his hands up. Kylee quickly changed tones.

"Alright let's go fishing," she said.

CHAPTER 7

Fishing was much better today. Between catching fish and talking about turkey frogs and kidnappings time flew by for the two fishing buddies.

"This is a lot more fun than yesterday; we should have tried this spot when we were here before," Kylee said as they sat in the narrow canal. She took a small perch off her hook and put it in a bucket with four others she had already caught.

"Yea, I guess the fish travel from one lake to the other through here. I never tried this area before, this is great." Justin said putting another worm on his hook and casting toward the shoreline.

"Hey! Look at those guys," Kylee said pointing through the trees as a couple of 4 wheel ATVs came into view.

"Wow! I wish we had one of those. We could

go all over the place." Justin watched as the two men on the ATV's drove up to the old hunting cabin and went inside. Kylee's eyes got as big as baseballs.

"Oops!" Justin looked at her. "I didn't think anyone used it anymore," he smiled at her.

"We're lucky we didn't get shot yesterday for being on their property," Kylee laughed.
Not long after the men went inside, another ATV came through the forest. The man on it was big and fat and wearing a sheriff's uniform.

"Uh oh, maybe they aren't supposed to be there either," Justin watched as the sheriff came to a stop.

"This should be good," Kylee said setting down her pole. The two men came out on the small porch.

"It shouldn't be much longer now," the sheriff said still sitting on his ATV.

"I don't like this," the taller of the two men said. He was wearing jeans and a red flannel shirt with the sleeves rolled up. "We need to get this over with as soon as we can."

"Listen Danny, you keep your mouth shut and do what ya'll are told or else. Do you follow me?" the sheriff shook his finger at the tall guy.

"Yeah yeah, we got it." The shorter of the two

men on the porch was shirtless and wearing a pair of blue jeans. "It's just more difficult than we thought it would be. That's all we're saying. Maybe if you could get us a little more cash it would ease our minds a little. You know what I mean?"

"A deal is a deal and you are going to hold up your end of this or you'll be in jail faster than you can say more cash! Got it?" The sheriff yelled, then started up his ATV and left quickly. The tall man kicked at an empty jar setting on the porch. It sailed through the air and busted when it hit a nearby tree.

"I wonder what that was all about," Kylee said.

"I don't know, but maybe we ought to get out of here." Justin watched the two men go back into the cabin, then started up the motor and pointed the little boat toward home.

"Justin put his fishing equipment away in the shed beside his grandmother's house and went inside. Lucille was sitting on the screened in porch when he walked in.

"How was the fishing today?" she asked, as Justin plopped down in one of the plastic lawn chairs.

"We caught quite a few today, but we let them

all go." He adjusted the ball cap on his head. "Hey grandma, who owns that old hunting cabin on the canal on the other side of the lake?" Justin asked.

"I didn't know there was a cabin along the canal. What side is it on?"

"It's on the right hand side going in," Justin said.

"Let me see, I know that property used to belong to Joe Boyer but I think he sold it to some guy who lives in New York. He was going to build a big winter home on it for him and his wife but she got bit by a mosquito and I don't think they ever came back after that." She laughed at the thought of someone buying land way out in the woods and thinking they wouldn't get a few mosquito bites. "Why do you want to know?"

"We saw a couple of guys over there today with a policeman and I was just wondering." Justin leaned forward and picked up yesterday's newspaper off the table.

"Was the sheriff a big fat guy?" His grandmother asked.

"Yeah, he looked like a pretty big guy." Justin studied the picture of Holly the Gator Queen again.

"You steer clear of that man when you can," his grandmother warned. "Sometimes he thinks he owns the whole county and don't always act the

51

way a law officer should." She stood up. "Do you want me to bring you out some lemonade?" She picked up her empty glass off the table.

"That sounds good." He set the paper on the table and leaned over it. His eyes were fixed on Holly's picture when she brought him his drink. She sat the glass down next to the newspaper.

"Grandma have you heard any news on the missing Gator Queen this afternoon?"

"No, just what we learned this morning that's all I know." She took a drink of her lemonade.

"Where was Holly at, when she got kidnapped?" Justin asked.

"She had just won the Gator Queen Pageant at the community center on highway 443. The air conditioner hasn't worked in that building for over two years and all those poor girls were dressed in their big hot formal dresses. She had just been crowned queen and had stepped outside to get some fresh air while the band set up on stage. But when they started playing and it was time for the queen to have her first dance, no one could find her," his grandmother said shaking her head. Justin sat back in his chair with his drink.

"Why do you think anyone would want to kidnap the Gator Queen?" he asked.

"It's all because of those greedy contractors who

want to turn this into a golf course community for the rich," she said.

"And what does Holly have to do with the builders?" Justin asked taking a long swallow of lemonade then returning his glass to the table.

"Well it's not so much her, as it is her sister Grace. She is the leader of the Church of The Turkey Frog. If they can get her to admit that there is no such thing as the endangered turkey frog then they can build all over this area. And Officer Brown, the man you saw in the woods, he will stop at nothing to help them because his great grandfather left him three hundred acres of undeveloped land on the east side of Crystal Lake over there." She pointed in an uncertain direction. "He stands to make a fortune if the deal goes through. Of course no one ever thought they would do something so crazy as kidnapping a young girl who hasn't hurt anyone."

"So it's possible he could be in on this thing?" Justin picked up the paper once more to look at the picture.

"Let's just say, I wouldn't trust that man to help me across the street." Justin looked at the close up picture of Holly again. She had a beautiful smile and a gold crown was resting on top of her long beautiful hair. Something in the lower left corner caught his eye.

"Wait a second." He looked at the picture closer. "I don't believe it!" He fought back the urge to yell, and got up and ran to the door.

"Where are you going? His grandmother looked at him. He turned around and ran back to the table. He picked up the newspaper and headed back out the door.

"I have to go see Kylee!" The door slammed behind him as he ran down the driveway.

"Hey Justin, I heard the fishing was pretty good today," Jack said when he answered the door.

"Yeah, we caught a few. Is Kylee here?" Justin asked standing on the porch.

"Yes, she's in her room playing with her MP3 player, whatever that is," Jack said. "Come on in and I'll go get her."

Justin waited just inside the door for her.

"Hey Justin, what are you doing?" she asked pulling headphones off of her head.

"Do you still have that pink thing you picked up yesterday at the cabin?" he asked.

"Yeah, but I don't think it will look good with that shirt you're wearing." she joked.

"I need to see it," he said quietly.

"Ok," she shrugged her shoulders. "We're

going to my room for a minute." she said to her grandfather who had sat down to watch TV."`
Justin followed her down the narrow hallway to a tiny bedroom.

"Here it is," she said untying it from around her bedpost. Justin opened up the newspaper on the bed and smoothed it out with his hands. He took the cloth from Kylee and laid it across the Gator Queen's picture.

"Look at that," he said taking a step back. Kylee looked at the bed and then at Justin, then back at the bed.

"Yeah, I see that's great. Thank you for showing it to me. Now, why don't you go home and get some rest." She put her arm around him to show him to the door.

"No look here," he said, pushing her arm away. "See her dress here on her shoulder. It's the same color as this." He placed the cloth across the lower corner of the picture. Kylee held her hair back with one hand and bent over the bed.

"So what does that mean?" she asked.

"It means Holly was at that cabin since she has come up missing. According to my grandmother, this is the dress she was wearing the night they grabbed her."

"We need to show this to my grandparents."

55

Kylee reached for the door knob.

"What do you think they will do?" Justin held her by her wrist.

"They will call the cops, that's what they will do." She looked him right in the eyes.

"We can't let them do that." Justin shook his head. "My grandmother told me that the cop we saw could be involved in this whole thing because he stands to make a lot of money if they get their building permits."

"Then who are we going to tell?" Kylee asked. Justin picked up the paper.

"Meet me at the dock at ten o'clock tonight. We need to find out for sure if we're right.

"My grandmother isn't going to let me leave this house at ten o'clock at night." Kylee sat down on the edge of her bed.

"My grandmother won't let me either, so we'll have to sneak out." Justin whispered.

"Sneak out! Are you crazy? Do you know what would happen to me if I got caught?" She stood again.

"Shhhh!" Justin put his hand over her mouth. "We have to act fast, and I don't think we should tell anyone until we know for sure."

"Do you realize I am a fourteen year old girl, and you want me to sneak out of the house in the middle of the night, get in a tiny little boat and go across an alligator infested lake, so we can spy on kidnappers who are already threatening to kill one teen age girl, and the only person that knows where I'm going to be at is a sixteen year old boy that's with me? That's what you want me to do?" Kylee was waving her arms about and pacing the room."

"I'd say that's pretty accurate," Justin nodded his head. Kylee stared at him and put her hands on her hips.

"Ok, ten o'clock," she said.

CHAPTER 8

Justin slipped out the back door at ten till ten. It was a full moon with a light breeze blowing in from the west. He looked across the street but his partner was nowhere in sight. Quietly he made his way down the dimly lit street toward Clear Lake not using the flashlight he had brought along. Justin stopped at the shoreline and looked back up the pathway but still no sign of Kylee. He stood in the darkness for more than a minute waiting, and wondering if he had the nerve to make the trip alone.

After five more minutes of standing around, Justin decided that the trip was too important not to go just because his partner chickened out. His shoes made a light thumping sound as he walked down the dock to the little boat. He got down on his knees and reached for the boat with his foot to pull it closer.

Save the Gator Queen

"It's about time; I thought you said ten o'clock." A voice came from inside the boat. Justin froze in fear for a split second.

"It's ten o'clock now. How long have you been down here?" Justin said getting situated in the back of the boat.

"I don't know, I thought I would practice sneaking out the window at about nine fifteen. But once I got out I couldn't get back in, the window is too high, I'll need your help later." She smiled but it was to dark in the shadows of the dock for Justin to see it. He turned on the flashlight for the first time, shining it at the motor to locate the choke and turned on the gas valve.

"I see you came prepared too," she said facing him.

"You brought a light also?" Justin would have been surprised if she had.

"Nope," she said, reaching into the pocket of her dark blue windbreaker, pulling out a large zip lock bag. "Beef jerky," she announced holding it up and shaking it. Justin shook his head.

"Why did you bring beef jerky?" he asked, not sure he wanted to hear the answer.

"Do you know how long beef jerky will keep?" she began. "If they catch us and throw us in a dungeon, we will be able to survive for weeks on this." She tucked it back inside her jacket. Justin had no argument for that line of thinking.

The sound from the small engine broke the stillness of the night and the two well-prepared heroes headed out across the dark waters. Justin guided them slowly down the narrow canal while Kylee held the flashlight beam of light steadily in front of them. He cut the engine and drifted along in silence.

"Cut the light," he whispered. Kylee turned off the light as the small cabin came into view.

"Look!" Justin said pointing up into the woods. The cabin windows were glowing with light from inside.

"Well, there you go. Now let's get out of here," Kylee said.

"We have to find out if Holly is inside there or not." Justin whispered.

"How about I'll holler for her and you see if she comes out," Kylee said, half joking. Justin stepped past Kylee after the boat came to a stop in the sand.

"No, you goofball, we have to get closer, come on." He stepped out of the boat.

"What's with the sudden burst of courage? I think the fact that someone is inside there is enough reason for us to let someone know they need to come out here and check it out." Kylee had not made a move to exit the boat.

"Kylee, come on. She needs our help." Justin waved her toward him.

"Oh, I get it now." She stepped to the front of the vessel. "My mother told me a boy will do anything for a pretty face. You like the Gator Queen, don't you?" She was starting to giggle. "I don't know why I have to risk my life because you think some girl is cute."

"Just come on," he said creeping up the slope.

"Ok lover boy, but if we get caught, the queen has to get her own food. I'm not sharing." She patted her pocket and fell into step behind him. He kept the light off most of the way, turning it on occasionally when they didn't know which way to go. When they reached the corner of the cabin, they could hear muffled voices coming from inside.

"I want to get a look in the window," Justin whispered and proceeded along the wall, Kylee stayed right behind him. Crouching below the window, they both raised up slowly to get a peek inside. The two men they had seen earlier were setting at the three legged table playing cards.

"I've got two pairs of three's," the shorter man said lying down his cards.

"That's four of a kind you moron," the other man said throwing down his cards

"So did I win, Danny?"

"Yeah Perry, you won." He pushed the small pile of coins across the table.

'Bam! Bam Bam!' Someone knocked on the door. Justin crouched down lower. Kylee fell over backwards clutching her hands over her chest.

"What do you want?" Danny stood up and grabbed a gun off of a shelf near the door.

"It's me, Ron. Open the door," the voice from outside yelled. Danny opened the door and the overweight sheriff came inside. He was wearing jeans and a light grey button-down shirt.

"We didn't hear you pull up," Danny said closing the door.

"I drove my truck. I walked in from the highway. Here I brought you guys something to eat." He handed over a couple of paper bags from a burger joint.

"Hey thanks." Perry said coming forward and taking the bags. Kylee got over her heart attack and peeked through the window.

"How is our little prisoner doing?" Ron waddled across the floor. Justin got closer to the window to get a better view. Holly was sitting on a chair with a piece of tape across her mouth and her hands tied behind her back.

"Is this really necessary?" Ron pointed at the tape.

"She's a lot like her sister," Danny said. "She talks all the time."

"Like her sister huh," Ron looked toward the ceiling. "Better keep the tape on," he said and tuned away from her.

"Any word on when we can release her?" Danny asked. Ron rubbed his chin.

"No, but if we have to kill her, I don't want it done here, understand?"

"Kill her?" Perry said with a mouthfull of cheeseburger. Ron walked over to where Perry was standing next to the table.

"That's right. Remember if they don't do what we asked, she has to turn up dead. That way they take us for our word next time. Piney Hillville will be built one way or the other." Ron was speaking louder then necessary. "But no bloodshed in this area, it will scare off future home buyers. I'll let you guys know when I hear anything from the turkey frog wackos, until then you guys just lay low." He then walked out the door and disappeared into the darkness.

Justin nodded in the direction of the boat. Kylee wasted no time heading away from the cabin. They didn't say a single word to each other until they had the little boat locked back up to the dock and they were walking up the path home.

"Well, now what do we do?" Kylee asked.

"I don't know. We can't go to the police because one of them is involved, and if we tell anyone else, they will form a search team and march in there and get Holly killed." Justin pointed a beam of light in front of them.

"I know who we can talk to. Jerky?" Kylee held the open bag up.

"Who? Justin said taking a piece of the dried meat.

"Grace Stevenson, Holly's sister. She is really cool and she could help us," Kylee said chewing on some jerky.

"I don't know, don't you think she's kind of weird?" Justin asked.

"Yeah, she may be a little odd, but it don't sound like we have a lot of choices do we." Kylee walked beside Justin. He turned off the light when they reached the street, both feeling a little safer the closer to home they got.

"I guess you're right, but how are we going to get in touch with her?" Justin reached for more beef jerky.

"I don't know, but I bet my grandmother can

tell me. I'll find out tomorrow," Kylee said as they stood in the street in between their two houses.

"Ok you find out and we'll get in touch with her in the morning. I'll see you then." Justin turned toward his grandmother's mobile home.

"Hey aren't you forgetting something?" Kylee said. Justin looked at her. "I need a boost."

CHAPTER 9

Kylee was sitting at the table the next morning eating a bowl of cereal when her Grandmother came back in from her morning walk.

"Good morning sweetheart," she said when she saw Kylee.

"Morning grandma," Kylee answered. "How was your walk?"

"Awful, just awful, Robin Whitman was out in her yard and told me she had heard that Grace Stevenson is going to the court house today to withdraw her statements about the endangered turkey frog."

"Why is that awful? That will get her sister back, right?" Kylee said.

"Yes, I guess your right. I'm just being selfish. I was only thinking about us losing our little home in the woods and everyone we know having to move away." Sheila poured herself a glass of orange juice.

"Where does Grace live at?" Kylee asking, hoping the odd question would not draw suspicion.

"Do you remember seeing a big nursery when your mom and dad brought you here? It's on the corner when you turned on to highway 443, about six or seven miles up the road." Kylee was asleep when they drove in, she didn't see anything. Sheila put the pitcher of juice back in the refrigerator. She took a business card off the door held in place by a palm tree shaped magnet.

"Here, this is her place." Sheila laid the card next to Kylee's bowl. The teen picked up the card and read it. Natures Treasures, Plants for all occasions, Grace Stevenson, Owner, followed by a phone number.

"Why do you want to know?" Sheila asked, sitting down across from her granddaughter.

"Oh, no reason. I was just wondering." Kylee laid the card back on the table. Her excitement was building inside her but she tried not to let it show.

"Well, I'm going to go take a shower." Sheila sat down her empty glass and headed down the hallway. Kylee grabbed the card and flew out the door as fast as she could. She went from a bowl of cereal to knocking on Justin's door in ten seconds flat.

"Justin, your little friend is at the door for you."
Kylee heard his grandmother call out. Justin
opened the door seconds later.

"I got her phone number," Kylee said, "but we
need to move fast. Grace is planning to go to the
court house today to admit that the turkey frog is a
hoax."

"Grandma we're going to my room," Justin
said taking Kylee by the arm and dragging her
across the screened-in porch and up the steps into
the house.

"Hello! Justin's grandmother," Kylee said having
no choice but to follow Justin. They didn't go to
his room though, they stopped in the kitchen and
he took the card from her. He laid it on the counter
and picked up the phone. Justin dialed the number
quickly. Kylee kept an eye out for his
grandmother.

"Nature's Treasures," a woman's voice came
through the phone.

"Yes, I would like to speak to Grace
Stevenson, please," Justin said nervously flipping
the business card over and over.

"This is Grace," She said. Justin swallowed
hard.

"Hi! My name is Justin Long and I have some
information about your sister," he paused but the

line was silent. "We don't know who to talk to because a law officer is involved with her disappearance."

"We shouldn't be talking on the phone," Grace said. "Where can I meet you?"

"Well," Justin had to think quickly. "Do you know where Shady Oaks Mobile Home Park is?" he asked

"Yes I know where it is." She answered. "If you drive to the back of the park near the lake, you will see a path that leads down to a boat dock. We can meet you there," Justin said.

"I'll be there in fifteen minutes," Grace said and hung up the phone.

"Go and get that piece of Holly's dress and meet me at the dock as fast as you can." Justin said. Kylee shot across the screen porch.

"Good bye, Justin's grandmother." She ran across the street and into the house past her grandfather.

"Hi, grandpa!" She ran into her room, grabbed the pink strip of cloth and ran back out the door. "Bye, grandpa!" By the time he looked up she was gone.

"Kid's today," he shook his head and smiled

Justin walked down to the dock nervous about what he was going to say to this strange woman he was waiting for. Kylee showed up at the same time he did. She had the cloth wrapped around her head again.

"Are we going to take her to the cabin right now? Hey! My grandfather has a gun, do you want me to go get it? Do you think we should make up secret code names so they don't know who we are? I bet Grace will put some kind of voodoo curse on them and turn them into chickens or something." Kylee was so exited she couldn't control herself.

"Kylee stop it!" Justin shouted, he pulled the cloth off her head and put it in his pocket. "I don't know what's going to happen yet, but if you don't be quiet you're going to be in the lake swimming for your life."

"Oh yeah, whatever!" Kylee said rolling her eyes at him. A red sports car pulled up and a woman got out and started down the path toward them.

"Uh oh, we can't go yet," Kylee said patting her pockets. "I forgot the beef jerky." Now Justin rolled his eyes at her. Grace approached with caution. Justin watched as the tall woman with long black hair looked around before approaching them.

"Did I just speak with you on the phone?" she said to Justin with a calm voice.

"Yes, you did. My name is Justin and this is my friend Kylee," Justin spoke. Grace watched Kylee as she stomped a bug dead on the dock.

"I've seen you some place before," Grace said looking at her.

"I was with the same search team as you the other day," Kylee answered. Grace nodded.

"Oh yes, that's where I saw you." She looked back at Justin. "So Mister Justin, what is this information about my sister you have?" Justin found it hard to speak.

"We know where she is," he finally said. "And we know who has her," he managed. Grace nodded her head.

"I see, well then where is she?" Grace removed her sunglasses a little suspicious of the two youngsters.

"We only know how to get there by boat." Justin pointed across the lake. "There is a small canal over there. Part of the way down it, is an old cabin. Two men are holding your sister there." He wondered if she believed what he was saying. Grace stared out across the lake.

"What is this you said on the phone about law enforcement being involved?" she seemed to be getting annoyed.

"We saw a deputy sheriff there too, and he

71

brought them some food." Justin could hardly breath he was so afraid of this person and had no reason to be.

"Listen kid, I think I know the cabin you're talking about, it's been empty for years. I appreciate what you are trying to do but I can't just go off chasing every wild story someone tells me. This is the life of my sister and I just can't fight it anymore. After today, they will get their permits and I will get my sister back. I don't know what you saw the other day, but I am sure it was not my sister." Grace put her glasses back on and put a hand on Justin's shoulder. "Thanks anyhow kid." Justin felt a rush of energy flow through him from her touch. After she started back to her car, Justin was able to speak again.

"What about this?" He held up the pink cloth.

Grace turned to him; she took her sunglasses off again when she saw the pink satin. This time she was speechless. She touched the cloth and Justin's hand started to tingle.

"Where did this come from?" she asked. Justin pulled a newspaper clipping out of his other pocket.

"We found it at the cabin. It matches this." He put it over the clipping in his hand much like he did in Kylee's bedroom the night before.

Save the Gator Queen

"Who all knows about this?" Grace looked Justin in the eyes. Justin was no longer nervous.

"Just the three of us," he said.

"The sheriff that brought them food, was he a big heavy man?" she asked. Justin shook his head as Kylee squashed another bug nearby.

"Yeah, that sounds like it could be the same guy," Justin answered.

"Ronald Brown. We want to be careful around him. He's a nut." Kylee laughed out loud thinking about how strange that statement seemed to her. Here is a woman that thinks a frog has magical powers and she is calling a county sheriff a nut. Justin and Grace both stopped their conversation to let her regain her cool.

"Sorry, it's just. Well you know the whole frog thing and all." She gestured with her hands. Justin and Grace stared blankly at her. "Just forget I even said anything." She went back to bug hunting.

"When we went there the first time, no one was there but we found this." Justin said.
"After I matched it up with the picture in the paper, we went back last night and that's when we saw her, your sister."

"How is she? Is she alright?" Grace asked.

"She seemed ok from what we could see. They had her tied to a chair," Justin said. He looked down at his feet. "What do you think we should do?"

"I want you to show me where this place is, and then we will come up with a plan." Grace replaced her sunglasses on her head.

CHAPTER 10

Grace stepped into the little boat gracefully. Kylee fell in like a ton of bricks almost tipping it over and Justin climbed in after making sure the boat was untied from the dock. It took a lot longer to cross the lake with another passenger. If we pick up Holly this trip the thing will probably sink, Justin thought as he listened to the small engine struggle.

While guiding the small craft carefully down the canal, Justin tapped Grace on the shoulder.

"That's the cabin right up there," he pointed.

"This is the Henderson property. They live up north. I'm sure they don't know this is going on," Grace said looking up and down the shoreline.

"Do you want to go ashore?" Justin asked. Grace didn't answer right away. The sound of another engine filled the air and a red ATV came into sight. Ron stopped his 4 wheeler about a hundred feet from the cabin, pulled out some binoculars and scanned the canal.

"Go! Go! Go!" Grace shouted. Justin maneuvered the boat into the direction from which they had come and gave it full throttle. The boat putted away slowly.

Justin was pulling back up to their home dock about thirty minutes after they had left it. Grace stepped onto the dock.

"Do you think they saw us?" Kylee asked.

"I don't know how they could have missed us," Justin said.

"Well, I believe they saw us but I don't know if he could tell who we were or what we were doing, so I wouldn't worry about it too much," Grace said knowing that Ron probably identified her but didn't want to worry her two young friends.

"Justin, would it be possible for you to have your boat sitting at the cabin tonight at midnight?" Grace asked. Justin broke into an instant sweat.

"Um yeah, I guess so," he finally managed to mumble.

"Alright here is the plan. Some of my followers and I will come in from the highway side under the cover of darkness. We will enter the cabin and overtake the two guys guarding Holly. When she is free, we will send her your direction."

"I have a flashlight I could signal her with," Justin said.

"Good, good, I'll tell Holly to go toward the light. This way when we leave the cabin, Holly will be out of the area. If we get caught, at least I will know she is safe. You bring her to this dock and I will pick her up here." Grace said.

"What about me, what do you want me to do?" Kylee said rubbing her hands together.

"Oh, well, um," Grace didn't think Kylee would want to be involved.

"She can help me with the flashlight and stuff," Justin said, seeing Grace's confusion.

"Ok good," Grace walked back to her car. "Don't do anything crazy now, just get Holly out of there, ok." Grace took Justin's hand. "And thank you, thank you both," she said looking at Kylee.

"We won't let you down, you can count on us," Justin said.

"Yeah together we are unstoppable." Kylee stood up straight and tall next to him.

"Good bye," Grace said driving away.

"Boy we are in it now," Kylee said, she slumped her shoulders. "How are we going to get the boat over there at midnight?"

"Just like we got it over there last night, how

else would we do it?" Justin said.

"So I have to climb out of the window again?" Kylee sounded frustrated.

"This time you don't have to practice, so don't climb out until you're ready to leave," Justin said. "Alright?" He bent down slightly so they were face to face.

"Yeah I know. You better not get us killed, or I will be in big trouble," Kylee said shaking her finger at him.

"Just be here at midnight, ok?"

"Yeah, yeah, yeah." She started up the path.

Grace pulled into Nature's Treasures and got out of her car.

"Did we sell anything while I was gone?" she asked Jeanie, who had been working for her since she opened up a year and a half ago.

"A guy came in and bought four hibiscus bushes but that's all," Jeanie said.

"Well, that's better than nothing." Grace was having a hard time trying to get her mind back on business. A sheriff's car pulled up to the nursery and parked. Ron Brown got out and walked between the different plants and bushes to the small building that was open all the way across the front. Grace met him at the entrance. He looked her up and down. She knew he was matching up her clothes with the person he had seen in the little boat a few minutes ago.

"What do you want?" Grace said with anger in her voice. He let out a soft laugh.

"It's about your sign, out front. It's too close to the road and we have told you before to move it," he said looking around the shop behind her.

"What are you talking about? No one has ever said anything to me about my sign!" she said.

"So you are denying you have been told to move it numerous times?" Ron said.

"I have never been told anything about my sign, because it is not in violation of the law." She put her hands on her hips.

"Well, I'm going to have to take you in and let you straighten this whole thing out in front of the judge." Ron reached over and picked a yellow flower off of a nearby bush.

"Stop that!" she said and grabbed his hand and took the flower from him. "Fine, I'll meet you at the court house." Ron looked at her fingers wrapped around his wrist.

"Assaulting an officer," he shook his head. "That's not going to look good to the judge." She let go of him but not before giving his arm a hard shove.

"Well, I believe you were going to the court house today anyway to settle a little misunderstanding about a frog, weren't you? So I think it would be best if I took you up there so we make sure both issues are solved." He reached for her hand and crumpled up the flower she was holding.

"Jeanie take care of the store, I'll be back shortly." Grace said over her shoulder. She followed Ron out to his patrol car and got in the back seat.

Sheila came out the door carrying her purse and car keys just as Kylee came walking across the lawn.

"I'm on my way to pick up a few groceries. Do you want to come along with me?" she asked.

"Sure grandma why not? We can't go fishing today until Justin goes and gets some gas for the boat." She walked around and jumped into the car.

Sheila stopped at the stop sign leaving the park as a police car drove by.

"Oh my gosh!" Sheila exclaimed. "That was Grace in the back seat of that police car."
Kylee had seen her also.

"What's going on?" she said. The highway was clear of traffic now but Sheila did not move.

"I don't know, but I am certainly going to find out." She turned the opposite way of which they were planning to go.

After a short trip they pulled into Nature's Treasures and parked next to Grace's car.

"We just saw Officer Brown drive by and Grace was in the back seat. What is going on?" Sheila asked Jeanie after they entered the store.

"I'm not sure. He said something about the sign out front being too close to the road and they were going to the court house to settle things," Jeanie said. Sheila looked out at the sign. Jack and Dewey Martin had put the sign in place a week before Grace had opened.

"It's the same sign that's always been there," Sheila said.

"I don't know what's going on. This is the first time I've heard anything about a problem with the sign." Jeanie said.

"Groceries are going to have to wait. We are going to see Mr. Martin and get to the bottom of this." Sheila turned Kylee around and went back to the car.

CHAPTER 11

Sheila turned off the paved road and drove a short distance around Crystal Lake to a big house up on stilts. They went up a flight of steps and knocked on the door. Soon a small man with a big smile appeared through the screen door.

"Hi Sheila! Long time no see. Come in, come in," he said opening the door.

"I'm sorry to bother you Mr. Martin, but I think something fishy is going on and I need to ask you a couple of questions." Sheila walked into the perfectly organized house.

"I'm retired; you're not bothering me, and please call me Dewey," he said.

"This is Kylee, my granddaughter from Pensacola," Sheila said putting her hand on Kylee's small shoulder.

"Well hello there, Kylee, would you like a soda? I have Sprite or Pepsi." He bent down to talk to her but didn't need to. He was only a couple of inches taller than she was to begin with.

"No, thank you," Kylee said with a smile. Dewey turned his attention back to Sheila.

"It seems like everything is starting to smell a little fishy around here lately and I'm not talking about the lake. What's going on now?" he asked.

"Well, we just saw Grace Stevenson in the back of Ron Brown's police cruiser." Dewey's eyebrows rose. "So we went to her nursery to see what was going on and Jeanie said that it was because the sign you and Jack put up is too close to the road."

Dewey didn't say a word. He walked across the big living room shaking his head. He sat down at a desk and opened the bottom drawer on the left. After shuffling through some folders he pulled out some papers stapled together. He laid them on the desk and quickly looked them over.

"Hog wash!" He spun around in his chair. "Right here is a copy of the sign permit. Grace had so much going on trying to get her store ready to open that I went and pulled the permit for her myself."

Kylee stood quietly; maybe this would be a good time to bring up the cabin and the plan they had in place to rescue Holly.

"Back when I was a judge, I did everything I could to get Ron off the police force. He's a no good scoundrel and if I could get a hold of him, I'd choke him to death." The skinny old man put his hands in a circle like he was choking someone. The papers in his hands crinkled as he shook them hard. His face turned bright red and big veins raised up on his forehead.

This may not be the right person to tell. Kylee thought.

"I think I better call up to the court house and see if there is anything we can do," Sheila looked at the wrinkled papers.

"It's no use," Dewey said leaning against the back of a couch trying to catch his breath. "Half the people down there are big supporters of his because they stand to make big money if Piney Hillville ever gets the green light."

"Then what are we supposed to do?" Sheila asked sounding frustrated.

"Let me make some calls to people I know down there and at least find out what's going on, then I'll give you a call. By the way how's Jack doing? I haven't seen him since the Gator Festival last year." Dewey walked them to the door.

"He's doing just fine, I'll tell him you asked about him," Sheila said.

Save the Gator Queen

"Tell him to come over here and we'll go fishing sometime." Fishing sure is big when there's nothing else to do, Kylee thought getting into the car.

"Kylee was sitting on the porch swing with her MP3 player on when Justin and his grandmother pulled in across the street. Justin opened the back door of the car and took out a gas can. Kylee met him at the end of his drive. The can was heavy and it took both hands to carry it.

"I think my grandpa has a wheelbarrow if you want me to go get it," she said sliding the headphones off her ears.

"No, that's all right. I got it," Justin said trying not to show he was struggling.

"Well, don't get in no big hurry because tonight is off." She reached in her pocket to turn off the music. "Grace is in jail." Justin dropped the can, a small amount of gas sloshed out onto the drive.

"What!" He couldn't believe what he was hearing.

"My grandmother and I saw her in the police car, then we went and talked to Mr. Martin who is a retired judge or something like that. He just called us right before you got home. Someone at

85

the court house said she has been arrested for assaulting an officer."

"I don't believe that, I bet that sheriff saw her in the boat this morning and he put her in jail because she knows where Holly's at." Justin sat down in the driveway and put his head in his hands.

"I'll go get the wheelbarrow," Kylee walked away. Justin tried to think of what to do now. If they saw Grace, then they also saw somebody else with her, so they will find a new place to hide Holly. Kylee came back pushing a blue wheelbarrow rocking her head back and forth to the music only she could hear. Justin set the gas can in it and they headed to the dock.

"I wish we knew how to get in touch with the Church of The Turkey Frog. If we could get in touch with them we could go ahead with our plan."

"Do you think a bunch of people that worship a frog are going to take a couple of kids seriously?" Kylee said putting her headphones back on.

"Hey kids!" Ron Brown was walking across the yard beside them. "Have you two seen a grey poodle running around here anyplace?" Justin dropped the handles of the wheelbarrow when he saw who was talking to them. Pam Slate who lived up by the park's entrance had lost her dog again and as always, called the sheriff's department to come and find it.

"What's the matter kid? Poodle got your tongue?" It was a stupid joke but it made him laugh.

"No, we haven't seen any dogs around here," Justin said, realizing that Ron had not recognized them. Kylee was dancing a few feet in front of him and was not aware Ron was talking to them. Justin caught up with her and grabbed her by the elbow. She turned around just in time to see Ron walking into someone else's yard, and then disappearing behind a garage. She took her headphones off.

"Did he see us?" she asked in shock.

"He was just talking to us, but I don't think he realizes we were the people in the boat with Grace." Justin looked at the MP3 player Kylee was holding.

"Muffin, where are you? You old flea bag," Ron called out from behind the garage.

"Can you record with that thing?" Justin asked. She had the cord wrapped around her neck and down her arm as she fought to get herself untangled.

"Can I do what?" she said, sticking it in her pocket again.

"Record, can you record voices with that?"

87

"Yea, I think so." She pulled the MP3 player out again and looked at it. "Yeah, this button right here," she said showing it to him.

"You keep an eye on him. I'll be right back. I've got an idea." Justin ran back to his house leaving Kylee with the wheelbarrow.

"If I could just find one normal friend, that's all I really want, is one." Justin was gone and she was talking to herself still tangled in her headphone cord.

CHAPTER 12

Justin ran into his room and took one of the speakers off the boom box he had brought from home. Stopping off in the kitchen, he grabbed a leftover pork chop out of the refrigerator and an aluminum pie pan from one of the cabinets.

"Do you want me to make you a sandwich?" his grandmother asked, seeing him run back out the door with the cold pork chop in his mouth.

"No thanks grandma, I'm good," he hollered back, heading for the shed. He grabbed a stringer and an old pocket knife out of his tackle box and shoved them into his pocket.

Kylee was standing right where he had left her when Justin got back.

"Where's he at?" Justin asked her.

"All you have to do is listen for a second," Kylee said and then cupped her hand behind her ear.

"Muffin! Where are you, you stupid mutt?" The voice came from behind one of the mobile homes nearby.

"Ah, there's the nice mister policeman now," Kylee motioned in the direction the voice had come from.

"Alright, let's go." Justin sat the stereo speaker in the wheelbarrow next to the gas can and the two teens headed in Ron's direction.

"Come this way!" Justin cut between two homes. He dropped to his knees and pulled a panel off one of the mobile homes that allowed access underneath it.

"Give me your MP3 player," he said. Kylee took it out of her pocket and handed it to him.

"What are you going to do?" she said untangling the wire again.

"I'll tell you if this works. Now I need you to go and find Officer Brown. Tell him we found Muffin and she is under this trailer."

"They don't like you calling them trailers; this is a mobile home," Kylee said putting her hand on the side of the home.

"Kylee, just go get Officer Brown and tell him about the dog." Justin played with the buttons on the MP3 player. She stooped down and peeked through the opening.

"Are you on dope? My mom said I can't hang around people who are on dope," Kylee looked at Justin.

"No, I'm not on dope. Now go get the cop."
"Ok, alright. There is a girl's life on the line here and we're chasing an invisible dog." She straightened up. "Oh I get it. This makes perfect sense now, and if I see Santa Clause or the Easter Bunny, I'll bring them back and we will have a tea party." She walked away mumbling to herself.

Ron was picking an orange off a tree in someone's yard when she found him.

"We found Muffin; she's over here under a house," Kylee said.

Ron looked at the orange and tossed it aside.

"Good, I'm sick of wondering around this dump." He wiped his hand on his shirt and followed her around the corner.

Justin was on his knees with the pie pan in one hand and the pork chop in the other.

"I brought you something to eat, come toward the shiny object." Justin was talking louder than necessary.

Yep, he's on dope; Kylee thought, when we get done here, he is on his own. I'm not hanging around with this kid no more.

"I once heard Mrs. Slate say that Muffin likes

shiny objects." He stood up as Ron and Kylee approached. Justin held out the pie pan and pork chop. Ron just looked at them.

"We saw her run under here right after we talked to you." Ron rolled his eyes.

"Give me that!" He grabbed the stuff out of Justin's hands and with a certain amount of effort, got down on his knees and stuck his head under the home.

"I got you something to eat, come to the shiny object! I got you something to eat, come to the shiny object! You dumb dog." Ron called into the opening. Justin smiled and backed away from the officer. Ron kept hollering for Muffin to come and get the pork chop. When Justin got to the end of the trailer, he shouted.

"Hey! There goes Muffin that way! How did she get out?" Ron scrambled to his feet.

"Are you kidding me?" he said struggling to his feet and brushing dirt off of his pant legs.

"Nope, I saw her, she went that way." Kylee motioned in the direction Justin was facing.

"She went under that silver car over there," Justin said. Ron walked as fast as he could still holding the pork chop and pie pan.

"Do you have any clue of what we are doing?" Kylee was truly lost, but was playing along with his crazy plan. Justin smiled at her.

"We just created the disturbance we need to save the Gator Queen.

CHAPTER 13

Justin sent Kylee home to get a mirror while he poured three gallons of gas into the boat's gas tank. He was playing with the MP3's buttons when she returned.

"Ok, here is what we are going to do." He took the knife out of his pocket and cut the plug off the speaker and stripped the plastic insulation off the wires. Then he cut the head phone cord in two.

"Hey! What do you think you're doing?" Kylee reached for her stereo.

"These two plugs are different." He held the head phone plug up next to the one on his boom box speaker. "I have to wire this speaker into your MP3 player for my plan to work." Kylee stared at him. "I can't ask the bad guys to put on the headphones now, can I?"

"I guess not, but I'm not happy about this and somebody owes me a new headset," she said folding her arms in front of her.

"Now here is what our plan is. We are going to put this mirror pointing toward the cabin. I rewound the tape to where there is about four minutes of silence before you hear Ron calling the dog." Kylee started nodding her head.

"I get it, they are going to think that stupid cop is bringing them lunch, and when they come out to get it, we'll beat them over the head with a tree limb." Justin waved his arms.

"Stop! Stop! Stop! You started out with the right idea. How about when they leave the cabin, we run in and get Holly, then head for the boat?" Kylee thought for a minute.

"Yeah, I guess that would work too."

They didn't talk much once the plan was in place as they crossed the lake once again. After entering the canal, both teens crouched down as the little boat glided into the sand covered shore. Justin picked up the MP3 player and speaker as Kylee climbed out of the boat with the mirror in her hand. This time they didn't head to the cabin, instead they made their way in a wide circle around it. Justin lined up a tall pine tree with the cabin and the sun. He set the speaker at the base of the tree and then he took the mirror from his partner.

"Barbie?" Justin said looking at the picture on the back side of the little round mirror.

"If you got a problem with Barbie use your own mirror," she smarted off at him. Using the stringer in his pocket he tied it to the tree up as high as he could reach.

"Are you ready?" he said. Kylee could not answer so she shook her head. Justin reached down and hit the play button. "Let's go," he said taking her by the hand, and heading back the way they had come. As they neared the cabin, Justin cut through the thick foliage to the side of the small house. They settled in quietly below the window and waited.

"I got you something to eat, come to the shiny object!" Ron's voice boomed through the forest. The sound of chairs scooting across the floor inside was followed by loud footsteps. The door swung open and two men came out onto the porch. Justin looked at Kylee.

"I got you something to eat, come to the shiny object!" The Mp3 player called out to the men.

"Boy, I hope he brought fried chicken this time," Perry said jumping off the porch.

"Wait a minute." Danny walked down the steps. Kylee closed her eyes. Justin felt like they could hear his heart beating. They watched as Danny walked past Perry.

"If it's chicken, I get the breast," he said and took off running.

"Hey, no fair, I get half." Perry gave chase as they ran from the cabin.

Justin slipped around the corner and was inside in no time flat. Kylee was only seconds behind him. Holly's eyes grew larger at the site of the two new faces. Justin quickly opened the pocket knife and went to work on the rope wrapped around Holly's waist holding her to the chair. Kylee took up a position just inside the door keeping an eye on the kidnappers.

"Hurry up!" she said.

"I'm trying," he said. "This is harder to cut than I thought." He sawed away at the rope.

"You better save some for me!" Perry hollered, gaining on Danny.

"Maybe it's ribs. I haven't had ribs in weeks." Danny jumped over another bush. Holly fell onto the floor as the rope finally broke free.

"Help me get her up." Justin grabbed Holly under the arm as she tried to get to her feet with her hands still bound behind her back. Kylee pushed the chair out of the way and took hold of Holly's other arm.

"I don't get it. Where's our chicken at?" Danny

stood scratching his head.

"Did you hide mine?" Perry said kicking at the bushes looking for his dinner.

Holly made it to her feet and out the door. Justin guided her toward the canal with Kylee bringing up the rear. Just as they reached the boat a gun shot went off. Justin pushed Holly to the ground. Kylee looked behind her as she ran and tumbled on top of both of them as they all rolled down the hill.

"They got me!" she said as she fell. Perry had his pistol pointed straight up in the air,

"If you don't give me my chicken right now, I'm going to shoot you in the foot!" Perry lowered the barrel of his gun. Danny put his hands up in the air.

"I don't have your chicken; I don't have any chicken see." The three teens rolled down the hill and crashed into their boat all wrapped up in Holly's pink dress. Justin reached over and pulled the piece of tape covering her mouth off.

"Are ya'll going to kill me?" She cried out. Justin was hurt by the thought of him doing any harm to the beautiful girl.

"No! No, we're trying to save you," Justin answered as she sat up and leaned against the boat.

"Well, try harder because you almost broke my

neck getting me this far." Justin took his knife and went at the rope binding her hands.

"Ok, ok. We'll try harder," he said. Kylee pulled off the pink fabric covering her head.

"You ungrateful pain in the….."

"Kylee! That's enough." Justin stopped her mid sentence.

"We are being shot at! I got a scratch on my arm and scraped my knee! My stereo is gone and I think I lost a shoe!" She dug around in the pile of teen aged bodies and pink satin before coming up with a red and white running shoe. "Ok, I didn't lose the shoe, but the rest of the story is true, and all we get is, try harder." She put the shoe back on.

"Danny! She's gone! Perry yelled from the cabin.

'What!" Danny had Kylee's Barbie mirror in his hand.

"She's not in here! She's gone!" Perry jumped off the porch looking around. Danny smashed the mirror against the porch post. Perry stopped dead in his tracks.

"Oh that's just great! Now we'll never find her. You just brought us seven years bad luck," he said.

"What would make you think we could find her anyway? We can't even find the food Ron left us."

He threw the plastic frame at Perry. Perry blocked it with his forearm.

"You owe me a new mirror too," Kylee said as they lay on their stomachs watching the two goons at the cabin.

"You two go get in the boat," Justin said crawling away from them.

"After you, my queen," Kylee said motioning Holly toward the boat. Justin untied the rope anchoring the boat to a fallen tree, then pushed it back out into the canal jumping aboard at the last second. Kylee was in her normal spot up front and Holly sat in the middle. Justin fought his way through her dress to the back of the boat and started up the little engine.

All three teens kept their heads low until they were out of the canal. Justin docked the boat quickly and they hurried along the Shady Oaks Mobile Home Park's dock.

"I don't want anyone to see me until I've talked to my sister and parents," Holly said. Justin stopped running.

"Why would that matter?" he said.

"Because I'm not sure who all is involved in this. I want to find out before someone who is in favor of Piney Hillville sees me and they call Sheriff Brown."

Save the Gator Queen

"Good thinking. Kylee go get something we can cover her up with and I'll go get the wheelbarrow." Justin started to leave.

"Why do I have to go find something to cover her up with? You're the one that thinks she's so beautiful. You go find something and I'll go get the wheelbarrow." Justin let out an embarrassing laugh.

"Stop joking around and go find something," he looked at Holly. She gave him a smile. Holly stepped back off the path while her two heroes went off in a hurry. Justin got back first and was wiping out the wheelbarrow with his hand when Kylee returned with a bed sheet.

"Ok Holly, hop in," Justin said. She gave him a look of doubt but sat down letting her feet hang over the side. Kylee covered her with the sheet and pulled on the front of the wheelbarrow while Justin pushed from behind until they got up on the pavement and things went a little easier.

"What are we going to do with her now?" Kylee asked.

"I don't know. I guess we'll take her to your house," Justin grunted as he pushed the heavy wheelbarrow.

"My house? I don't want her at my house! What if they are following us?" Kylee ranted on.

"Do you know how much trouble I'll be in if some psycho gang comes crashing into my grandparents' house because of something I drug in I shouldn't have?"

"Well, I can't take her to my house because I'm not allowed to have girls in my room." Justin said trying not to tip Holly out onto the road.

"Hey guy's, I can hear ya'll," Holly said from under the sheet. "Just get me somewhere that I can use the phone."

"Look!" Kylee said as they turned onto Seagull Lane. "Your grandmother's car is gone. We can take her there long enough to make a couple of phone calls."

"I don't know." Justin sat the wheelbarrow down; "If she comes home and catches us, I won't be able to go fishing the rest of the summer." Kylee rolled her eyes.

"You were willing to risk us getting shot at but you're afraid of being grounded." She flailed her arms about.

"Hey kids, what have you got there?" A man watering his lawn came over to them. All three of them looked his way even though Holly's head was covered.

"Oh, it's a, it's a." Justin stuttered.

"It's a German Shepherd." Kylee said.

"Oh yeah, why do you have its head covered up?" The man reached for the sheet. Kylee quickly stepped in between him and the wheelbarrow.

"Its eyes are sensitive to the light, umm, it was a seeing eye dog for years. Now it just don't want to look at nothing anymore." She hung her head.

"Oh I see. Well you kids be good and don't get into any trouble," he said and went back to his yard work.

"Oh no, don't worry about us," she looked at Justin. "We would never do anything that might get us into trouble."

"Seeing eye dog?" Justin looked at her.

"I didn't hear you come up with anything smart guy." Kylee walked ahead of him. Justin picked up the wheelbarrow and headed for his grandmother's driveway.

CHAPTER 14

Justin opened the door and let Kylee guide Holly into the living room. Holly pulled the sheet off of her once she was inside.

"Where's the phone?" Justin handed her a cordless phone off the end table. She dialed a number quickly,

"Hi mom! It's me," she said after a few seconds.

"Where are you? Are you alright?" her mother asked.

"Yeah mom, I'm ok. Some kids rescued me today and I'm at the Shady Oaks Mobile Home Park. Can you come get me?"

"I don't know if that's a good idea or not. Sheriff Brown has arrested your sister and some guy is sitting out front watching our house all the time. Can you stay where you are for awhile until we can get things worked out?"

"Why is Grace in jail?" Holly asked.

"Nobody will tell us but we have a pretty good idea. They want her to drop the whole turkey frog endangerment thing so they can run us all out of here and build their big golf course city. Let's not worry about that right now. We need to work on getting you home. Call me back in an hour and I will see if I can get someone to come and get you."

"Ok mom, but hurry. I miss you."

"I miss you too honey," her mother said as Holly hung up the phone.

"She can't come and get me because they have our house staked out," Holly said turning toward Justin.

"Well, what are we going to do now?" he said. The door knob rattled, but the door didn't open. Kylee grabbed the sheet and tried to put it back over Holly's head, after all she was the one they wanted.

They had tried, it had been a great effort and they almost pulled it off, Justin thought. The door rattled again before opening.

"Justin, would you get this darn wheelbarrow out from in front of the door? I almost dropped my groceries trying to move it," his grandmother said stepping through the door with her arms full of plastic bags. She froze and two of the bags hit the floor when she saw Holly.

"Oh my God, Justin! What have you done?" she screamed.

"Grandma, it's ok, I'm not the kidnapper," Justin said, tossing the sheet onto the couch. The color had left Lucille's face. "We found her out in the woods. Can we keep her?" Holly looked at him.

"I'm not a stray dog," she said.

"I meant just for right now," Justin tried to defend himself.

"He means he loves you and wants you to stay forever." Kylee put the sheet around her neck like she was in an old romantic movie.

"Hold it, hold it, someone needs to explain to me what in the world is going on here." Lucille felt like she was going to faint and they were joking around.

The teens realized the seriousness of the situation and went into action. Holly brought a chair out of the dining room and set it behind her. Justin and Kylee helped guide her onto it.

"Holly, are you alright?" Lucille asked, putting her hand up to Holly's cheek.

"Yes ma'am, I'm ok. I've called my mother, but she can't come get me because they are keeping an eye on her," Holly explained. "I'm going to call her back in an hour and see what she can work out." Lucille put here hands in her lap.

"You are welcome to stay her as long as you need to," she replied. Kylee punched Justin in the arm and leaned over and whispered in his ear.

"It's like a dream come true, isn't it?" Justin put his hand over her face and pushed her away.

Lucille made sandwiches and lemonade for the three of them as they talked about the unbelievable stunt they had just pulled off. When they finished, Holly called her mother back and was informed that Jeanie would come by at five o'clock and pick her up. She would be able to stay a few days with her until things got ironed out. Lucille took the phone and gave directions to her home.

Ron pulled up to the cabin on his ATV.

"How is our little captive doing today?" he said when he saw Perry and Danny standing on the porch.

"We got a bit of a problem," Danny answered walking down the steps.

"What kind of a problem," the smile fading from Ron's face.

"She got away! Somebody came in here and helped her get away," Danny said. Ron couldn't believe what he was hearing.

"What do you mean somebody came in here. Who?"

"We don't know….," Danny was cut off before he could finish

"What do you mean, you don't know? You were here the whole time!" He looked in the door, then turned and faced his men again. "You were here the whole time, right?" Danny looked at Perry. "You were here, weren't you?" Ron walked over to Danny.

"Yeah, we were here, but well, they kind of tricked us. They are super intelligent whoever it was," Danny said.

"I bet it was Grace Stevenson. She's real smart," Perry added.

"It couldn't have been Grace, because I just got back from putting her in jail." Ron was furious. "We have to find her or we are in deep trouble. She knows who we are and if she starts blabbing off, we could have some serious problems. So how did they get her out of here without you two stopping them?"

"They had this recorder over there next to a tree. We thought it was you bringing by some sandwiches or something."

"We were hoping it was chicken," Perry

added. Danny took off his cap and hit him with it, and then he handed the recorder to Ron. He studied it for a moment then pushed the play button. His voice came through the speaker. Ron threw it against a tree busting it into a hundred pieces.

"We've been outsmarted by a couple of kids." He stared down the canal. "I want you two over at the Shady Oaks Mobile Home Park in five minutes. We are going to knock on every door until we find those two. A blonde girl about thirteen years old and a boy with dark hair, looked to be about sixteen. They shouldn't be hard to find, there can't be that many kids in that broken down old folks dump." Danny and Perry stared at him. "Move, now!" Ron shouted and peeled out on his ATV.

"Lucille called Kylee's grandmother and told her what had happened and that the kids were all right.

"Oh my!" exclaimed Sheila. "What have those two kids gotten themselves into?"

"Sheila don't worry, they're alright and they have Holly with them," Lucille said.

"Yes I know that, but I talked to Pam on the phone a few minutes ago, and she said some men were just at her house asking about a couple of kids."

"Oh no!" Lucille found a place to sit down.

"She said they looked pretty rough, so she said she didn't know of any kids staying in the park." Sheila peeked out the window.

"She lives up by the gate, doesn't she?" Lucille asked

"Yes, just as you pull in; she's there on the right."

"Listen, here is what we are going to do. Get out your park directory and we will call everyone in the park, starting near the gate and tell them to say they don't know anything about the kids," Lucille said.

"Good idea. I'll take A through M and you call N through Z so we don't call the same ones," Sheila said.

"Ok, got it." Lucille hung up the phone. "You kids go in the back bedroom and close the door."

"What's going on?" Justin asked.

"There's some guys in the park that are looking for you three," Lucille said.

"I think I better go home," Kylee went to the door. Lucille stepped in front of her.

"No! You can't go outside or they might see you. Your grandmother knows where you are. Now you kids do what I said." She gently guided them down the hallway.

"Come on guys." Holly said, "This isn't a game, let's go hide." The three of them walked down the hall to the back of the mobile home.

"Yes, I have seen some kids around lately. Morton, whose grandkid is it that you saw fishing the other day?" Morton Smith was asleep on the couch in his home next door to Pam's. "Excuse me just a minute the phone is ringing." Morton's wife told Perry as he stood on the Smith's porch. He smiled as Mrs. Smith came back to the door.

"I don't know of any kids!" She said and slammed the door in his face knocking off his baseball cap.

CHAPTER 15

Lucille and Sheila kept at the phones for nearly an hour before there was a knock at Lucille's door. Lucille peeked out the window; she saw a police cruiser sitting in the driveway.

"Hello officer Brown," she said as she opened the door. The two had a history as did most people in Shady Oaks Mobile Home Park with Ron. None of them were very good. He was pushing hard for Piney Hillville, and no one in the park wanted to give up their homes to a big developer.

"Hello Mrs. Long! How are you this beautiful day?" he said removing his hat.

"I'm fine, what can I do for you," Lucille said.

"Well, we received a report that a couple of teens have stolen Mr. Preston's boat and I wondered if you knew where I might find them." Ron talked like they were old friends.

"They didn't steal anything; Mr. Preston gave

them permission to use his boat."

"Ah so you know who they are, and one of them is your grandson isn't it!" He pushed past her and entered the home.

"Oh my," she said covering her mouth. He stormed down the hallway opening the doors as he went. Lucille chased after him.

"Hold it right there!" She screamed holding a knitting needle in her fist. "You don't have a search warrant." Ron slowly walked toward her.

"I don't need a search warrant." They stood inches from each other in the narrow hallway. "This is personal business." He took the needle out of her hand and bent it in half. Ron slammed open the last door at the end of the hall. No one was inside the bedroom. Ron opened the closet door so hard it bent the hinges. He stuck his head inside it, rifling through the clothing. Lucille stood just inside the doorway. Kylee gentle pushed the door from the other side. When Lucille saw her, she stepped forward to allow Kylee to slip down the hallway.

"Ron you stop that, I want you to get out of my house!" He left the closet and opened the small bathroom door. He pulled back the shower curtain, jerking it off its rod. He was surprised to see nothing but a bottle of shampoo and a half used bar of soap.

Lucille noticed a piece of pink satin sticking out of the antique cedar chest that set at the foot of her bed. She quickly opened it, tucked the fabric inside, and then took a seat on it.

"I will find those kids, and I will hold all of them until someone puts an end to this endangered turkey frog business! You mark my words!" He screamed and stormed out of the house. Kylee came in from hiding in Justin's room.

"The coast is clear," she said. Justin fell out of the tiny linen closet behind the bathroom door. Lucille stood up and helped Holly out of her hiding spot.

"Kids, I'm so sorry. How could I have been so dumb?" She was disappointed in herself for letting him search through the house.

"It's alright grandma." Justin put his arm around her. "That part is behind us now."

Across the street, Sheila was on the phone working on her own plan.

"Dewey they have Grace in jail," she said into the phone.

"Jail! On what charges?" he said surprised.

"I don't know."

"That's it! That is it! I am going to Ocala and

putting a stop to this whole mess. I'm putting a stop to all of it; Gator Queens, innocent people in jail, golf course communities, kidnappers, and chicken frogs."

"It's turkey frogs," Sheila corrected her old friend.

"Whatever it is, I will stop it all!" he said and hung up the phone. Sheila laid the phone back on the table. That did not go the way she had hoped. Her phone rang while she wondered what to do next.

"Sheila, it's Dewey, I forgot I don't drive anymore. Could you run me to the court house?" He had calmed down quite a bit.

"Sure Dewey." She tried not to laugh. "I'll be right over."

Dewey marched into the court house like he owned the place.

"I want to talk to Sheriff Clark," Dewey said to the receptionist.

"I'm sorry sir but the sheriff is in a meeting. Can I set an appointment for you at a later date?"

"Honey, I started the 'tell them I'm in a meeting line.' You tell Chuck that Dewey Martin is here to talk to him." Something in the small man's action caused her to fumble around with the

115

phone until she was able to dial the sheriff's office.

"Sheriff there is a Dewey Martin here to see you. I told him you were in a......yes, sir...... yes, sir...... alright...... yes, sir," she hung up the phone and cut her eyes up at Dewey.

"Right down this corridor, go to the third door on your left, sir." She pointed to a hallway behind her. Dewey gave her a smile.

"Thanks hon. I knew you could help me." He winked at her as he walked by. "Chuck will get this straightened out." Dewey held the door for Sheila.

"I can't believe they let that idiot run around in a uniform with a gun." She headed down the hall next to the fired up little man.

"Dewey, how have you been?" The sheriff came around the desk, reaching for Dewey's hand.

"I am fed up, that's how I am!" Dewey didn't take the sheriff's hand. "We are living under a constant fear in our part of the county and I am telling you right now I will not stand for it one more day." He was calm and cool but more forceful than Sheila was comfortable with.

"Well now Dewey, let's sit down and talk about what's bothering you." Chuck sat down behind his desk.

"I don't have time to sit down and be treated

like a two-year-old child. There is an innocent
woman in jail and three teenagers who are trying
to do the right thing, and they are being hunted like
deer." Dewey paced back and forth as he talked.

"Well then, what is the name of the woman in
jail and I will pull up her record?" Chuck hit a few
keys on his keyboard and concentrated on the
computer screen on his desk. "And we'll get a man
out to check on the teens." Dewey leaned across
the desk and hit the power button at the bottom of
the monitor. He looked Chuck straight in the eyes
and spoke in a calm, steady voice.

"I told you she is innocent. So there is no
record, and the teens are hiding from one of your
men. Now you are going to call the jail and have
Grace Stevenson released." Dewey walked behind
Chuck's desk. "And then you are going to take the
badge away from Officer Ron Brown. Do I make
myself clear?" Dewey placed his hands on the
arms of Chuck's chair. The sheriff looked over at
Sheila. Dewey put his hand on Chuck's chin and
turned his head until the two men were eye to eye.

"I'm right here Chucky. Do we have an
understanding? I may not be a judge anymore but I
am the same person I have always been, Chuck.
We wouldn't want any of our little secrets to come
up from the past now would we? If I'm not

117

mistaking this is an election year, isn't it?" The sheriff shook his head the best he could with Dewey still holding onto his face.

"Make the call." Dewey released him and handed him the phone from the desk. Chuck looked at Sheila again then took the phone. Sheila was speechless and could not believe what she was seeing.

"Yes, this is Sheriff Clark. I want Grace Stevenson released to Dewey Martin right away." He paused momentarily, "That's correct, Mr. Martin will be there shortly." Chuck hung up the phone and faced Dewey who was now seated next to Sheila.

"Is this about Piney Hillville and the permits they are trying to acquire?" Chuck asked.

"Yes, it is." Dewey answered. "I have stood by quietly up 'til now on the issue because when a person, or a company in this case, follows the laws of this great country, I am all for progress even if it inconveniences me. But when they break laws and bribe the people who are to uphold those laws, somebody has to stand up for what is right." Dewey put his skinny forearms on Chuck's desk and leaned forward. "I was a judge for thirty one years Chucky. I followed the law when the law was right; which was almost all the time. But on occasion I had to do what was right when the law was wrong, didn't we Chuck?" Chuck hung his head slightly and gave a nod Dewey's way. Sheila sat still feeling like she was hearing things she wasn't supposed to hear.

"In all those years I made thousands of judgments and I have not regretted a single one. Don't make me change my mind." Dewey stood to leave. "Let's go Sheila." He placed his hand on her shoulder.

They walked down the hall and out to her car without a word. Sheila started the car.

"Dewey, how did you do that?" She asked.

"Do what?" he said.

"Get Sheriff Clark to do whatever you wanted." Dewey cocked his head sideways as if looking at a distant memory.

"When I first met Chuck, he was a rookie officer fresh out of the academy. Someone had bought the house next to his grandmother's on the west side of Ocala." Dewey smiled. "The old woman would bake two dozen cookies and make three gallons of Kool Aid every day. Then she would set up a table on her front porch and lay out her goodies. When the neighborhood children got off the bus, they would go to her house. They would eat and play games in the front yard, and she would sit in a lawn chair and watch them until their parents came by to pick them up."

Sheila drove the short distance from the court house to the county jail while listening to Dewey's story.

"It was kind of like a free daycare and it gave the old woman something to live for. Well, the new neighbors wanted it stopped because she didn't have a license for a daycare." Sheila parked in the parking lot as Dewey continued.

"Sometimes you have to do what's right when the law is not. Chuck's grandmother could not afford to file all the proper paperwork, not to mention understand the mountain of junk. So we produced a license by the next morning. It may not have been done according to the law but it was the right thing to do. After that, he and I worked together on a lot of situations like that." Dewey opened the car door, but didn't get out right away. "When he ran for sheriff, I was his biggest supporter. He's a good man Sheila, but we have done some things that could have got us both in a lot of trouble over the years. I'm not saying we were wrong, I'm just saying they weren't exactly legal either."

CHAPTER 16

"Thank you so much, Mr. Martin. Thank you." Grace said, hugged him again.

"Don't thank me, a couple of kids went out there and got her," Dewey said. She pulled back again.

"Justin and Kylee?" she asked.

"Yes, how did you know?" Sheila looked puzzled.

"I met them this morning, are they all right?"

"Yes, they are fine." Sheila led the way back to her car.

Holly was helping Lucille with some microwave popcorn while Kylee and Justin were watching TV when someone knocked on the door. The three teens quietly moved to the bedroom while Lucille went to the door.

"Grace, it's you! Oh it's good to see you!"

Lucille waved Grace, Sheila and Dewey into her small living room. The teens came out of hiding when they heard the friendly voices.

Holly and her sister embraced tightly for over a minute. Grace broke the hug when she opened her eyes.

"And you two." She tried to sound angry, but the laughter and tears kept that from happening as she wrapped her arms around them both at the same time. It was hard to move in the small room full of people. A loud speaker from outside stopped the celebration.

"Anyone who is caught hiding the two youths who were trespassing on private property will be prosecuted. The Stevensons want the release of their daughter immediately. We have strong evidence that the kidnappers are in this area. Please be on the lookout for a young girl in a pink dress. Should you see her, please contact the authorities." Ron drove by slowly in his police cruiser talking into the PA system.

"That guy has lost his mind," Dewey said.

"I'm scared," Kylee said.

"We'll take you to our house until we can get the law back on our side," Grace said.

"We can't," Holly said. "I talked to mom earlier and they are watching the house. We can't go back there. Mom called Jeanie and she is going to let me stay at her place for awhile." Grace shook her head.

"Lucille, Lucille." Grace was looking around at all the faces in the room, "Can I use your phone, I have an idea."

"Of course dear, it's right over here." Grace called the nursery.

"Nature's Treasures," Jeanie said.

"Jeanie, this is Grace. I want you to close up shop early and get over here to Shady Oaks."

"Are you at Mrs. Long's house with Holly?" Jeanie asked.

"Yes I am. Also, there is a big white box on the bottom shelf behind the coke machine that I want you to bring when you come." Grace hung up with Jeanie and started dialing another number.

Fifteen minutes later, she hung up the phone for the last time after calling everyone in The Church of The Turkey Frog.

Danny sat behind the wheel of his truck at the end of Seagull Lane waiting for something to happen.

"Hello beautiful!" he said, as Jeanie drove past in her Jeep. Two other cars passed by not long after.

123

"There seems to be a lot of people gathering at 2510 right around the curve on the left," Ron said, pulling up next to Danny's truck and rolling down his window. "Drive down there and see if you can spot them kids."

"You know, I was just sitting here thinking," Danny said. "If we don't find the Gator Queen and your people don't get their building permit, then we don't get paid do we?"

"That's exactly right, so get over there!" Ron yelled. Danny remained calm.

"Well, it seems to me that this is turning sour. There is nothing to keep us from taking off and getting out of here before things get really bad. What do you think Perry?" Perry was watching two squirrels running up and down a tree nearby.

"Whatever you say boss," he said not paying attention. Ron shook his head.

"Yep, you're right. There is nothing to keep you here." He started to drive away. "Oh except the Gator Queen can identify you both and I'm an officer of the law. I could have you locked up by nightfall if you two don't do what I say!" Danny looked at Perry who was now alert.

"Good point," Danny said. "We're on our way."

Save the Gator Queen

Grace opened the box Jeanie had brought. It was full of black hooded robes much like the ones many of the people arriving were wearing.

"Holly, you Justin and Kylee find a place to sit." They did as they where asked. Justin sat down on the couch as someone in a black robe with their face covered sat down beside him.

"This should fit you," Grace said, walking past him and dropping a robe in his lap.

"Turn and face me," a voice from under the robe beside him said. He looked and saw a jar of white make-up in their hand.

"Oh no! oh no you don't! I'm not joining a cult!" Justin scrambled to his feet.

"Relax," Grace touched his arm. "We are just going to get you guys away from here for awhile." Justin saw white makeup going on Holly's face. Kylee was laughing as a man smeared the white goop on her cheeks. The person beside him lifted the hood off their head. It was a young woman about the same age as him with long red hair.

"It's ok," she said smiling. "See we are just like you." She unzipped her robe. She was wearing a green shirt and blue jeans. Justin looked her up and down.

"See, nothing to be afraid of." She took the lid off the jar and dipped a finger into it. She reached up and touched him on the nose leaving a white finger print.

"Stop it," he said wiping it off. "I don't believe in flying frogs and turkeys hopping around on four legs with magical powers."

"Oh, I don't blame you there, that would be plain ridiculous." She smiled. "My name is Marla. What's yours?" She held out her other hand; Justin didn't answer the thin, pretty red head. She touched the make up to his nose again.

"Has a turkey frog ever hurt you?" she asked.

"No," Justin smiled at the stupid question. Marla smiled back.

"Has a turkey frog ever made fun of you?" Marla rubbed more make-up onto his forehead. Justin let out a laugh.

"No," he answered.

"Has one ever stolen anything from you?" Justin looked into the eyes of the pretty girl and shook his head no. She dipped into the jar again and put both hands on his face.

"Has a turkey frog ever…" She paused. "Saved your grandmother's house?" Justin turned cold. His eyes darted around the room at all the different people, then his eyes met hers again.

"I believe in the turkey frog?" Justin took hold of Marla's wrist. "I believe in the turkey frog." He looked deep into her green eyes and then slowly stood up.

"I believe in the turkey frog!" he yelled.

"Did you hear that? What a bunch of maniacs," Perry said, as he and Danny sat in their truck at the end of Lucille's driveway.

CHAPTER 17

"Hey Ron, you may want to get over here."
Danny said into the two way radio in his truck.

"Why? What's going on?" he asked.

"I don't know, I think someone has died or
something." Danny said watching as seventeen
people all dressed in black hooded robes walked
out of the mobile home in a long line and headed
up the street.

"I'll be right over." Ron put his car in gear and
headed for Seagull Lane. The string of The Church
of The Turkey Frog was a block down the street
when Ron pulled his cruiser to the front of the line
and got out.

"Hold it right there." Everyone in black
stopped walking. Sheila ran up to the car with
Dewey and Lucille close behind.

"Isn't it beautiful?" she said. "The Church of
The Turkey Frog is practicing for the Gator Parade

tomorrow."

"You cannot hold a parade without the proper permit." Ron walked over to the parade leader and pulled off their hood.

"Hello Ron! How are you?" Grace said. Ron thought his eyes were going to pop out of his head.

"What! How did you?" The rest of the parade began to surround the policeman.

"The power of the turkey frog got me out of jail," Grace said. Ron backed up against his cruiser as the sea of black closed in around him. "I was ready to give up and withdraw my request for the turkey frog to be on the endangered list, but since I have my sister back and you threw me in jail, I am now more committed than ever to stop Piney Hillville from happening."

"It's over Ron," Dewey said wading through the group of turkey frog believers. "Chuck knows what you have been up to."

"This is not over, you will all have to move. Piney Hillville will be built, frog or no frog!" Ron got into his car and sped off. Jeanie pulled up behind him and stopped; she hopped out of her Jeep and found Grace.

"Do you still want me to take the kids to my place?" she asked.

"I think for tonight it would be a good idea

since Ron and his morons don't know where you live." Everyone agreed and Holly, Kylee and Justin jumped into Jeanie's Jeep.

"I'm still working on Tommy's costume for the parade, maybe I'll bring it over later and we can all work on it together," Grace said

"Ok, that should be fun," Jeanie said, climbing behind the wheel.

"Grace, if it's alright with my parents, could you stop by and pick me up. I'd like to help work on the costume too," Marla said while smiling at Justin. He smiled back.

"Sure, I guess you can never have too much help. I don't see why not." Kylee leaned over and whispered in Justin's ear.

"Uh oh, now you have to choose which one you're going to act like an idiot for, Red or the Queen." Justin didn't comment he just kept smiling at Marla.

After a few minutes, everyone had managed to get back to their cars and drive away. Sheila, Lucille and Dewey were standing in Lucille's driveway when Chuck Clark stopped by.

"Have you seen Officer Brown?" he asked from behind the steering wheel. Dewey laughed.

"Yeah, we've seen him. He was just here trying to find the Gator Queen. He was not happy to see

Grace Stevenson out of jail." Dewey leaned against Chuck's car.

"I've been trying to radio him ever since you left my office, but he won't answer." Chuck said.

"He left here a few minutes ago, I'm surprised you didn't see him on your way in," Lucille said. Chuck tried to get him to answer the radio as they stood there.

"He won't answer. I guess he realizes I'm going to ask for his badge. Not answering isn't going to help him, so I don't know why he is doing this."

"Because he is a nut and you should have never been put on the force. I knew the first time I ever saw him he was crazy but I didn't think he would try to hurt children the way he has." Lucille ranted; of course it was not the first time Chuck had heard such complaints about Ron.

"Well, if you see him again, tell him I'm out here looking for him. I will not stand for any of my men to abuse the authority of the Marion County Sheriff's uniform. You folks have a good day," he said and drove away.

"It looks like we may be on the track of getting to keep our homes after all," Sheila said.

"Yeah, thanks to Grace." Dewey put his arm around his friend.

"And a small group of kids don't forget,"

Lucille added.

"How did our grandchildren get involved in this mess so quickly?" Sheila asked.

"I don't know. Justin is not the adventurous type. This is completely out of character for him," Lucille said. "And Kylee seems like a nice quiet child also." Sheila laughed.

"You don't know her very well, do you?" Sheila invited them both to her house for iced tea.

Just as the sun set, Grace and Marla came to a stop in front of Jeanie's house.

"Run up to the door and have them come out and help us." Grace said opening the trunk of her car. Marla came back with Justin and Holly and they began loading up their arms with bags of feathers, a large fiber glassed frog head and body, some cardboard cut out in the shape of wings and a half dozen other things that were too difficult to describe. Soon it was all spread out throughout Jeanie's living room and dining table.

"Where did you get this?" Kylee said, her voice was muffled by the large smiling frog head resting on top of her shoulders. Grace smiled and lifted it off of her.

"I have a friend that works at a theme park in Orlando; this is something they were not going to use anymore so he got it for me." She set the head down on the floor.

"So what are we going to do with it?" Holly asked. Grace picked up one of the trash bags full of chicken feathers and one of the giant cardboard wings.

"We are going to glue these feathers onto these wings and attach them to the back of that frog body." She pointed to the biggest piece lying on the floor.

"This just stood on the sidewalk at the theme park, like a statue, so we have to make it where it can be worn by a person. I have some canvas that I think we can make the legs and arms out of, so Tommy can walk around with it on." Grace pulled some heavy green material out of a box. "I guess a couple of us could work on the legs and two of us on the wings."

"Justin and I could do the wings," Marla said quickly and looked at Justin.

"Oh please," Kylee rolled her eyes.

"Alright and Holly and I will work on the legs," Grace said. Jeanie called out from the kitchen.

"I've got pizzas in the freezer. Who wants some?" Everyone did.

"I'll help Jeanie," Kylee said going into

133

the kitchen.

The work continued into the night as everyone was having a good time putting the frog together. Grace was so happy to have her sister back that Holly had to tell her to back off several times. Justin could not walk across the room without Marla right behind him and he seemed to like it that way.

The clock on the wall was in the middle of its twelve chimes when the head was lowered onto the body with Kylee inside. Holly was closer to Tommy's size but Kylee liked putting on the get up and Holly would rather not.

Kylee managed to take three steps before she toppled forward. Grace, Justin and Holly were there to catch her. This was not the first trial run for the costume, but it was the farthest Kylee had gotten so far without crashing to the floor.

CHAPTER 18

It was a beautiful Florida day as the sun filtered through the forest. Jeanie was frying some eggs when Kylee woke up on the couch. It wasn't long before Justin came to life on the living room floor and Holly stumbled out of Jeanie's spare bedroom.

"Good morning turkey frog builders," Jeanie laughed. Holly scanned the messy house they had caused. Hot glue guns on the table, scraps of canvas and cardboard on the floor and chicken feathers everywhere.

"Morning," Holly said, picking a few of the items up. Justin got to his feet and started putting feathers in an empty box. Jeanie put breakfast on the table as the phone rang.

"Hello," Jeanie said.

"Hey Jeanie, it's Grace. So how did everything go after I left?" Grace asked

"It all went fine. We're just waking up."

Jeffery Lamb

"I have to take the costume by Tommy's this
morning. Tell Holly I have her blue dress with me
for the parade. I'll be by around ten."

"Ok, I'll let her know. See you later. " Jeanie
hung up the phone and sat down at the table.

"That was your sister. She is going to bring
your dress by for the parade and I am going to take
you two home right after we have breakfast," she
said to Justin and Kylee.

"I'm home," Kylee hollered out as she burst
through the door of her grandparents' house.
Sheila was standing in the living room wearing
blue jeans and a red flannel shirt with a yellow
hard hat on her head.

"Hi honey! Did you have fun last night?" she
asked. Kylee looked at her grandmother funny.

"I had a great time, why are you dressed like
that?" she giggled.

"It's for our float. We are representing death to
Piney Hillville." Sheila held out her arms and spun
in a circle.

"I don't get it," Kylee said.

"I told you, Mr. Ross has an antique hearse.
Well, your grandfather and I are construction
workers and we are going to ride on the hood like
we were run over. Then the rest of our group is

136

going to walk behind the hearse cheering instead of mourning. We have a banner on the car that says "Piney Hillville rest in peace." Jack came in from the porch. He had stuffed a pair of pants and shirt with newspaper and put a styrofoam head in the neck of the shirt making a fake person.
Both Jack and the dummy were wearing hard hats as well.

"You guys have lost it. Does mom know you do stuff like this?" Kylee smiled, she knew her grandparents were not like most, and deep down she was proud of that fact.

"I have one for you out in the shed," Jack said knocking on his hat.

"No thanks, Holly said Justin and I could ride with her since she wouldn't be here if it weren't for us," Kylee said.

"Oh that is wonderful! You get to ride with the queen of the parade." Sheila pinched Kylee's cheeks.

Grace parked her little red car in Tommy's driveway and went up and knocked on the door. Tommy was twenty four years old and had lived in the area about three years. It was just after he had bought his house that he heard that a big contractor wanted to wipe out the area by building a big

137

housing development nearby. He had heard that
the only thing holding up the plan was a bunch of
nuts that called themselves The Church of The
Turkey Frog. It sounded like a good way to meet
other people in the area and to help save his home,
so he found out where they met at and he had been
an active member ever since.

"I got your costume in the car," Grace said when
he came to the door. "You want to give me a hand
with it."

"Sure," he said and followed her to the car.

"Boy it's bigger than I thought it would be,"
Tommy lifted the fiber glass body out of the trunk.

"That's good," Grace said taking the head out
of the back seat. "That way everybody will be able
to see you," she laughed.

"Yea, I guess I'll be pretty hard to miss," he
laughed.

"Ok then, I guess I'll see you at the fire station
in about an hour." Grace said and laid the frog
head on Tommy's porch.

"I'll be easy to see, I'm pretty sure of that," he
smiled. Grace got back in her car and headed to
Jeanie's house. Tommy looked at the large
costume.

"Oh boy, what have I got myself into this
time?" he said to himself. "I wonder how hard

that's going to be to walk in." He stepped into the body and pulled it up onto his back. It was big and bulky but it didn't weigh much. He walked around the porch without much effort. Going down the steps was much harder, but he managed. Tommy picked up the frog head and put it over his. This made it somewhat more difficult; walking straight wasn't too bad but when he wanted to turn, he had trouble seeing where he was going.

"I'm here to turn you into a queen," Grace said when Holly came running out the door. She was wearing a pair of sweat pants and a t-shirt that Jeanie had let her borrow.

"Good, I can't wait to get this over. I never wanted to be the stupid Gator Queen anyway," Holly said. Grace stepped back surprised.

"Holly, you don't mean that." She handed the dress to Kylee.

"Yes, I do. I would rather be in jeans riding through the woods on my four-wheeler than putting on all this junk." She held up an eyeliner pencil and then tossed it on the coffee table with all her other make-up. Grace raised her head with pride.

"You just remember, if it wasn't for a certain Gator Queen, you wouldn't be able to ride your

ATV anywhere. All your trails would be part of a golf course."

"I know, I know but you're different. You were able to make a difference, you spoke up for things and people listened to you." Holly sat down and looked at the carpet. "I don't think I'm the Gator Queen type." Grace sat down beside her sister.

"Gator Queen is what you make it Holly. I did what I thought needed to be done; you have to do what you feel you need to do." Grace looked at her sister surprised at how she was growing into such a beautiful woman. "Gator Queen is just a title. You are still Holly Stevenson just like you have always been." The two sisters hugged each other as Jeanie wiped a tear from her eye.

Tommy decided he had had enough practice with the costume and was convinced he would make a pretty good turkey frog. He turned so quickly to his left that it threw him off balance, the heavy frog head tilted forward and he had to run to keep from falling flat. Now bent over running through his front yard, he could not see where he was going. Crash!

Tommy slammed into the side of his house. He fell onto the ground, surprised he was still breathing. The giant turkey frog slowly sat up then stumbled to its feet. Tommy pulled at the head but couldn't get it off. It had jammed itself down onto the frog body. Tommy tried again.

"Help!" he screamed. No one heard him but the echo inside the fiberglass head almost punctured his ear drums. "Calm down, calm down Tommy," he told himself. "I'll just wear it to the parade" He went to get in his car but he couldn't sit down with the frog suit on. Tommy went up the steps to the house so he could call someone but was unable to talk on the phone because of the giant head.

"Help!" This time he said it just to himself. He had almost an hour before the parade started and the fire station was only a couple of miles from his house. The only thing left to do was walk.

Sheila was putting some extra tape on a banner on the side of a 1959 hearse when she saw Grace coming toward her.

"Have you seen Tommy?" she asked.

"No, I haven't seen him." Sheila straightened her hard hat.

"I dropped a costume off for him awhile ago; he should have been here by now," she said looking down the road.

"Grace!" A woman came running up wearing a black robe. "Come quick Robert's truck is overheating and that is who was going to be driving Holly."

"If it isn't one thing, it's something else," Grace said and followed the woman toward the rear of the parade line up.

"Ok, when the parade comes around that curve, I'll block the road with a tree." Ron said, sitting on a narrow dirt road off Dear Creek Road. Danny and Perry were next to him in their truck listening closely. "Once it stops, you will fall a tree across the road behind them," he said to Perry. "Danny here will grab the Gator Queen and head to Orlando. I'll pick up Perry and we will get a hotel room until they meet our demands," he smiled. "And they will be much higher than before." His smile turned into a laugh.

CHAPTER 19

The Gator Parade started on time but the overgrown turkey frog was nowhere in sight. Grace had arranged for Holly to ride in Jeanie's Jeep. The Gator Queen was always the last car in the parade.

"Is everyone ready to go?" Dewey walked across the fire station parking lot. He was wearing lime green walking shorts, a bright yellow button-down shirt with red, white and blue suspenders. He had on black socks pulled up almost to his knees with white running shoes and dark sunglasses with a straw hat. Somehow it didn't look to bad on the skinny old man.

"We're ready when you are," Sheila called out from the hood of the hearse. Jeanie shook her head that the Queen-mobile was ready to roll. Dewey made his way to the front of the line and climbed onto his three-wheeled bicycle.

"Here we go!" He tooted a horn on the handle bars and began peddling. Behind him was Brownie troop 64 which consisted of two mothers and seven young girls in their uniforms. The fire truck was supposed to be next in line, but it had a flat tire so all the volunteer firemen were in the back of a four-wheel drive Dodge pickup. The Church of the Turkey Frog, with Grace leading her black hooded followers, minus Tommy and the Frog suit was next. Six golf carts, two clowns and the local Boy Scout troop followed. The Shady Oaks hearse came next, then Four World War II Veterans in a red Buick convertible, eight people on foot from the Moose club and then Jeanie's Jeep. Three dogs ended up in the parade too, sometimes behind the Jeep, sometimes in front of it.

The parade stopped not long after it started when it turned off the highway. Deer Creek Road had a small slope to it and Dewey had to get off his bike while two of the Brownies helped him push it up the hill, but soon they were off again.

Justin was surprised to see how many people were lined up along the dirt road to see the short mass of silliness go by. Families stood out by their mailboxes and waved and shouted as they slowly passed. Kylee would wave like crazy to the people and then settle down until they got to the next mailbox. It was a lot more fun than either one of them had expected.

They rounded another curve in the winding road and Dewey brought the line up to a halt. A tree was blocking the road at a part where no spectators were nearby. The volunteer fire department jumped off their Dodge and with axes went to work on the tree. As they were getting in the full swing of things, some of the other people from the parade were helping by dragging the limbs they had cut off to the side of the road, when another tree fell behind them.

"What's going on?" Grace pulled back her hood and walk toward Jeanie's Jeep.

"Boy, that was close," Jeanie said looking at the tree almost touching her Jeep. Dewey rode up to the two women on his bike.

"Are you kids alright?" he asked. Holly, Kylee and Justin all shook their heads and climbed out of the back seat. A black pickup came flying up the road and skidded to a stop on the other side of the fallen tree. Danny jumped out wearing a Halloween mask that looked like a psycho clown. It had long red hair and big blood shot eyes.

"Nobody move and no one will get hurt!" he shouted holding a shotgun down by his side. Perry came stumbling out of the woods holding another clown mask in his hand.

"The queen here is going with us," he said, grabbing Holly and trying to put the mask over her head.

"The mask was for you, goofball," Danny shouted at his partner.

"Every time I swung the axe it covered my eyes, Danny." Perry said putting the mask on top of his head and pulling it down over his face. Danny shook his head.

"You didn't need it then, you need it now!" He was trying not to lose his temper. "And I told you not to use my real name." Perry lifted Holly over the fallen tree. Grace saw something coming up the road behind Danny. It looked to be about the size of a motorcycle.

"Wait! Don't take her, take me instead." She thought if she could stall them long enough, whatever it was she saw might be coming to help. Perry stopped half way over the tree.

"Oh, I don't know about that. Ron told us to bring back the Gator Queen."

"Again with the names," Danny said.

"I didn't say Danny, I said Ron." Perry looked at Danny and saw the same thing that had gotten Grace's attention. "Hey, what is that right behind you?" Perry pointed.

146

Save the Gator Queen

Tommy had been trapped in the frog suit for over an hour now and was exhausted; he just didn't think he couldn't take another step.

Danny turned around as a huge turkey frog fell into his arms and knocked the rifle out of his hand. The over sized frog head butted against his and knocked him unconscious. Grace and Justin hurdled over the tree in one jump and wrestled Perry to the ground. Holly fell to her knees and grabbed the gun.

"Oh, I have been waiting for this you scumbag." She pulled it back like a baseball bat and hit Perry right across the jaw. A puff of clown hair floated up as he hit the dirt.

Ron came running up out of breath.

"Everybody freeze." He had both his pistols drawn. "Drop the gun my little queen and go with the nice men." Holly lowered the rifle and Perry slowly got back to his feet and took hold of her arm again.

"Ron, stop it right now, it's over and you lost," Grace said.

"It's not over until I see Piney Hillville covering this neck of the woods and all of you lowlifes are out of here!" He pointed one of the guns at Grace. "I am the law out here and you all will do as I say."

147

Danny came to and saw the giant frog staring at him.

"They're real, the turkey frogs are real!" He screamed, still recovering from the blow to the head. Tommy just stared at him while Dewey walked over to the back of the hearse.

"What was that again Ron? I'm a little hard of hearing." He put one hand on the back door of the car and the other he cupped around his ear.

"I said I am the law in this area and what I say goes!" He screamed so everyone would hear this time. Dewey swung open the back door of the hearse and pulled back the dark blue curtain.

"I don't think that is the way it works in this county," Chuck Clark said getting out of the car to everyone's surprise but Dewey's.

"I had a bad feeling about today," Dewey said.

"As usual, you were right, your honor." Chuck shook Dewey's hand. Holly and Justin jumped back onto the good side of the tree. Marla in her black robe was there to make sure Justin was ok. Perry almost fell over the tree. He had been leaning on Holly more than keeping her from getting away. Kylee hopped up on the tree face to face with him and grabbed his shirt collar with both hands and shook him.

"Where is my MP3 player? Do you have it?"

she said.

"Kylee, Kylee calm down, we'll get you a new MP3 player." Holly helped her little friend down.

"I don't want a new MP3 player, I want my MP3 player."

Two sheriff cars came up the road and loaded Danny, Perry and Ron into the back seats and drove away. The firemen went back to work on the fallen trees and soon the parade continued.

Later in the afternoon, the small parade pulled back into the fire station.

"This is the best parade I have ever seen, and I was in it." Kylee jumped off the Jeep before it stopped.

"We don't normally have this much excitement," Sheila said as everyone began to gather and talk about what had happened.

"I'm just glad everyone is safe," Grace said taking off her hood.

"Well it looks like that's the end of Piney Hillville," Dewey said pulling his bike up to the crowd. "Have you really seen a turkey frog or has that all been just a hoax?" Grace looked him in the eye. Three firemen were behind Dewey trying to get Tommy out of the frog suit.

"Of course it exists, because if it didn't, we

would all have to move away from here and I'm not going any place. Are you?" Dewey shook his head.

"No, I guess I'm not." He smiled. "Thanks to the turkey frog." Holly came up behind her sister and gave her a bear hug.

"I promise to be the best Gator Queen I can and make you proud."

"I'm already proud of you and I am sure you will be a great queen." Kylee ran up to Justin.

"That was a lot of fun, wasn't it?"

"Yeah, it was pretty cool," he said. Marla was right by his side.

"You want to go fishing later?" Kylee asked. Justin looked at Marla; she scrunched up her face like she had just eaten a lemon.

"I don't think I'll be doing much fishing this summer," he said as Marla leaned over and kissed him on the cheek.

Jeffery Lamb lives in Central Florida with his wife Sherri and their two dogs. He has a true passion for the sunshine state and its mix of interesting people.